St. James Way

By
John McCarthy, MD

Case ID: 1-14997922931

Paperback: 978-1-969775-04-8

LCCN: 2025921190

Introduction

by the Author

This book was written over 8 years ago.

It has a topic of the Mideast conflict that is threatening a world disaster. I wrote this book mainly to remember my older brother, James Richard McCarthy, who died age 19 of complications from a neurosurgery. I was 16 and loved him. He was having grand mal seizures throughout his teenage years and wanted to stop them. He continued to be a good student, varsity football (3 years) player, guitarist in a band, and my loving older brother. I questioned all meaning in life after he died. My writing in this book about spiritual themes is sincere. We humans have the power to destroy life and/or to grow into more loving and wise beings.

With free will we get to choose a way. Can humans find the way to grow? The book is my effort to share with the reader my thoughts and feelings about our journey in life. Love and wisdom give us purpose to grow.

JEM, MD (2025)

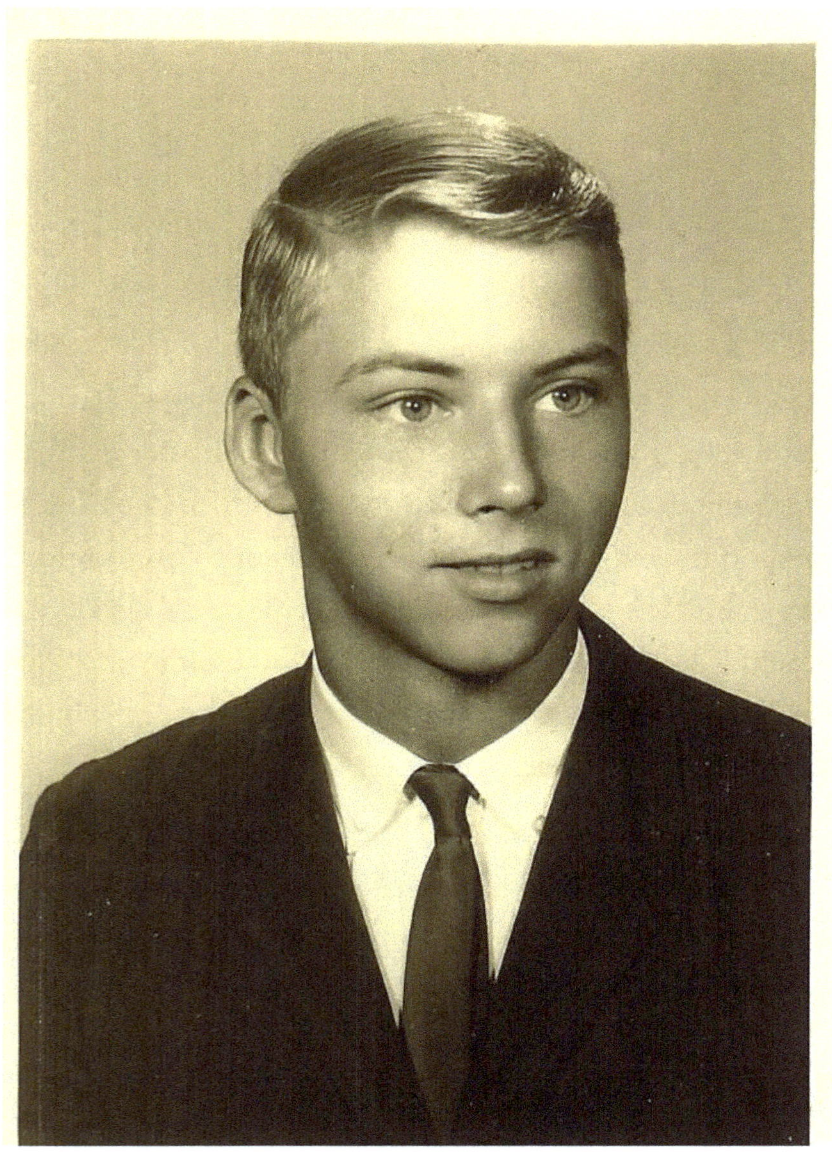

James Richard McCarthy, age 18 (Rick)

4

Dedication

To My Brother
James Richard McCarthy

(1947-1967)

Table of Contents

CHAPTER 01 | THE OZARKS

Time began along that gurgling stream in the silence of the pine tree canyon. It was a half-century ago. His brother's line whirled over the water and landed on a swirling pool. Something missed it, disturbing the surface.

"Try again," said George.

He did, and a bat nearly caught the fly just as it touched the water. Damselflies and tiny bugs darted across the sparkling stream. Suddenly, the pool erupted—an angry trout had taken the hook.

"He has it now," yelled Ricky. "It's a brook trout."

Not so big, but full of fight. Ricky pulled it in.

"Nice one, Rick."

They were alone, surrounded by the sheer white and coffee-cream walls of the Ozarks. They always released the fish. It was tired, and Rick said, "You're a beautiful trout. Go home now." It seemed to understand and quietly, gratefully waved its tail goodbye.

The stars appeared, the sweet cool breeze announced twilight. Camp was a stone's throw from the stream. One could hear it as it caressed their suburban ears. Rick and George came here for the peace and freedom from the family home near Chicago. Rick had a gift for music and often played the guitar after the dishes were washed and the dark night enveloped the canyon. George sang along with Rick that night, "Puff the Magic Dragon." Actually, they both carried a tune well. The campfire reflected off Rick's face.

They slept in a roomy canvas tent on six-legged cots. As the waters tumbled along the smooth stones, George wondered about creation. The peace and beauty of the forest comforted him.

Rick said, "I love the Ozarks and want to stay here. Home is Mom screaming and fighting with Dad. I never get a seizure here."

Rick had epilepsy due to an AVM in his brain. Next year it got worse, and he had to quit football—too much head contact. Two years later, he had surgery to remove the arteriovenous malformation. He died the day after the surgery due to a massive hemorrhage.

When Rick died, a big chunk of George's faith in God turned to anger and resentment.

What is the point? Nineteen, strong, courageous, loving, musical, and handsome. Now gone. Are humans just toys the Creator has forgotten?

One positive note: Rick could have died in Vietnam. Instead, he bled out in the same hospital George barely survived in ten years earlier when he had meningitis.

That was the last trip to the Ozarks they took together. Rick was cremated, and there was no funeral service. He would later visit George a couple of decades later.

George was living in Florida at the time the visit happened. He was awakened in his bed. His medical training was finished and started a new job as a psychiatrist in a small community along the east coast of Florida. He had gotten married. Ann was drinking again and depressed. He had long days and nights with his mentally ill patients. No one really taught George about alcoholism, and he really wasn't sure it was a disease. He wanted out of the marriage.

It was a frightening dream. George heard something. He looked up from his sweaty pillow. Some glowing light was there.

"It's gonna be okay, George."

"Is that you, Rick?"

"I love you, George."

Later he asked Ann if she had heard or seen anything.

"No, I was hungover. Dead to the world."

"I saw Rick last night. He told me he loved me."

Ann said, "You were having a bad dream."

"Yeah, I was. Then he was there, and I felt such relief."

CHAPTER 02 | FLORIDA

For a while after the divorce, he missed Ann. Work and making money and peace around the house got him over it. He enjoyed his work. He liked mentally ill people who wanted to get better—people trying to do life. His two cats, watching college football on TV, and gradually drinking more found him a happier person. He moved into a bigger home, a better office, and met women.

During his training, he had several years of psychoanalysis. His analyst at one point suggested he try a gay relationship.

"You might like it."

George was very disappointed with this. Overall, he had respected the man who had helped him further his professional life. After that, he had decided to pursue women and quit psychoanalysis.

He wanted children and a loving, sexy wife. Yet there was a persistent fear.

George was afraid of women and did not trust them. He thought that eventually they would try to destroy him. It was easy to blame Mother. She scared the hell out of all of them. But as time went on, the fuller meaning of the fear and anger with women became clearer. His drinking was accelerating too.

On the east coast of Florida, hurricanes will visit. One summer, three came by his home. It was invigorating to sit in the lanai by the pool as the wind roared overhead. He had his cups filled, and the cats ran for cover under the bed. He loved it. Happily high in defiance of nature, he sat while the storm beast blew away trees and roofs. His home was spared. No damage. No flood.

By now the booze was taking its toll. He decided to take a vacation. A trusted former patient, Cindy, had a small business of babysitting pets and house cleaning. She was married and a mature Christian woman. She attended church regularly. She offered to take care of the cats whenever he was gone for any extended time. He chose Cancun for his destination.

He missed the flight due to traffic on the way to Fort Lauderdale Airport. Hell with that. He had not drunk in months. But now he was on vacation. Stupid is as stupid does. He bought a bottle and then found a hotel. Time to kill. He wanted to see the beach. So he drove on the causeway toward the beach.

He had to go through a toll gate to get to the causeway. Strange to see that. The booze hit him then. He had not eaten and was feeling drunk. After a half mile, he decided to turn around. Better hide the bottle in the trunk. He pulled over and put the bottle in the trunk. There. When turning to get back in the car, a big guy jumped on him. Mace was sprayed in his face too. He was blinded and screaming. It was the cops. So he went to jail.

The Broward County jail holding tank had about ten men in it. They were mean, and were screaming out. The cell was about 12 by 12 feet and had one filthy open toilet. Somebody was looking for a fight. It was a memorable, terrifying, humiliating night. But George was alive. This was to be a major turning point in his life as a doctor and a responsible citizen.

So much for Cancun. As he left the jail, he noticed a lawyer's phone number posted for legal assistance. Strangely, he was allowed to drive himself home. The car had been impounded in a remote towing lot in Hollywood. Seething with anger and battling a brutal hangover, he paid the $200 towing fee. The bottle of booze was still in the trunk. George drank it on the way home.

By some surreal guidance, he got home safely. Cindy had cleaned the house and fed the cats. She greeted him at the door.

"You look awful. And why are you here? You should be in Cancun."

"I decided not to go," he mumbled. "I need to take a shower. Get cleaned up."

"Let me just finish up in the kitchen," Cindy said.

"No, that's okay. I'll be alright."

"I will wait for you to see if you are okay." She would not take no for an answer.

Revitalized from the shower and another shot of elixir, he entered the bedroom. She was lying on the bed in only her bra and panties.

"Come over here, George. I mean Dr. Elliott."

"No, you're a former patient and a married woman. Please leave."

"Come here, George, and rest a bit. Tell me what happened."

His towel was still around him. He went for some clean underwear. She caught his hand and pulled him onto the bed. She kissed him and said, "What happened?"

He told her. The faint scream of a man in the holding tank sounded in his mind.

So it goes. The pleasure of lustful sex with a psychiatrist's "Thou Shalt Not" made it even more pleasurable. She also liked it too much. She became more than a friend.

"I like you more when you drink," she said.

So he drank when she was around. However, the state monitor for doctors who were in recovery was looking over his shoulder. George made the decision to go to more meetings, stop all drinking, and say "no more" to her.

Still, the damage was done. The consequences were set in motion. His ability to practice safely was compromised. He chose to enter a program for troubled doctors in Gainesville.

CHAPTER 03 | FLORIDA

At the rehab center, the medical director greeted each new patient with a warm welcome. He began, "This is the love you need." But few seemed to believe him. The language of recovery—honesty, openness, willingness—was shared and repeated, but remained abstract for many.

A few days into treatment, a young doctor, beginning her first rotation in an addictions fellowship, took George's medical history. During the interview, he admitted to a prior relationship with a former patient and a DUI in South Florida. Eventually, this information made its way to the state medical board. The outcome was severe: first a suspension, and then the permanent loss of his medical license. The case sparked debate over how boundary violations should be handled.

***

George spent six months at the recovery center. Though he entered the program voluntarily, he experienced it more like a prison. When he left, he was sober—but burdened by heavy debt, unemployable due to the loss of his license, and unsure of what lay ahead.

One thing kept him grounded during his time there: a book. *Autobiography of a Yogi* by Paramahansa Yogananda sparked something in him—a sense of hope, a fascination. The book offered focus, sanity, and mystery. George found himself wondering: Was the author telling the truth?

One story in particular stuck with him. The author claimed that his teacher—long deceased—had appeared physically in his room, congratulated him on his spiritual progress, and said he now lived on another planet where he helped a humanoid civilization navigate political challenges. Then, the teacher vanished.

Despite everything, George clung to the possibility that the story was true. In those pages, he found something he hadn't felt in a long time: Hope.

***

Eventually, the center discharged George. Months later, while still struggling to reestablish his career, he failed a routine drug screen. The test was positive for oxazepam, a mild anti-anxiety medication prescribed by his regular physician. George rarely took it and didn't particularly like it. He had believed that, with a doctor's prescription, it was allowed. But the monitoring program had different rules. And rules were rules. The failed test sealed his fate— his medical license was permanently revoked.

***

The Department of Health employed prosecuting attorneys tasked with removing unfit doctors. George's assigned prosecutor was diligent and committed to the mission. George, by contrast, was broke and unable to find legal representation. In the end, he had met his match. Accepting defeat, he decided to move back to Alabama, where he had gone to engineering school.

Truthfully, he didn't go back to start over. He went back to drink.

CHAPTER 04 | ALABAMA

Stop that self-pity. Gloria was his neighbor in the small east Alabama town he now called home. She was a big, generous, good-natured lady. She could sing gospel like Aretha, cook delicious southern fried dishes, and they were friends.

"I just love you, George."

"I love you too, Gloria. Like a friend."

They would laugh and sing together. They shared life stories. Sometimes he would put on a Barry White album. George could get the mood and say, "Oh, baby!" real down deep. She would let go of a wonderful laugh. "Ooohh."

George began to get fat on soul food and booze. Sometimes the self-pity and depression would get him down. He had to go in the hospital for a few days then.

***

The twelve steps and meetings were few and far between in rural Alabama. He met several doctors in recovery there. The Deep South was not well connected to the program. The doctors would meet in the cafeteria of the hospital. George found these intimate gatherings really helpful. He attended regular meetings as well. They shared their experiences and feelings. George found his sobriety came more easily, and it was appreciated.

Although science and medicine still have a limited understanding of addiction, research suggests that dopamine plays a key role—specifically, that it is either insufficiently present or poorly utilized in the brain's limbic system. Other neurotransmitters, such as GABA and serotonin, are also believed to be involved.

People struggling with addiction often experience persistent feelings of restlessness, irritability, and dissatisfaction. Chronic worry and sadness are common, and individuals may become overly sensitive, withdrawn, and emotionally reactive. However, when they use their substance of choice, these negative feelings temporarily subside.

Addiction frequently runs in families, indicating a combination of genetic, psychological, and socioeconomic influences. The brain's pleasure and reward centers are central to this disorder. Studies have shown that direct stimulation of these reward pathways can produce pleasurable feelings and relieve depression—sometimes diminishing the individual's urge to seek out external sources of pleasure, such as drugs.

CHAPTER 05 | FLORIDA

The lurking black dog of despair and melancholy began to fade away. Somehow the program of spiritual life opened his mind and heart to fresh air and clear light. Faith in a God of his understanding gradually grew. Don't worry, have a little faith. He who was sold on the scientific method had fallen into an empty, meaningless castaway existence. Now how ironic that spiritual sustenance could begin a gradual journey back to life. Religious efforts had always driven George crazy. Letting others give to him when they could, while loving them in return when he could, was working. And faith in an unseen loving spiritual friend became easier.

A woman entered George's life—her name was Maria. They met in London during the spring and explored the city together. She was from Spain and spoke no English, but George knew some Spanish, enough to connect. Their romance continued even after they returned to their respective countries.

Maria had bright brown eyes and a soft voice, especially when she sighed. She trembled when she cried. George was tall and thin; Maria, of average height for a Mediterranean woman, had dark hair and skin lighter than his. There was a quiet steadiness in her Spanish manner, a constancy he admired. Still, her fears could loom large, like monsters in a child's closet. She was stronger than she realized—and, if it came to it, she could outrun him.

CHAPTER 06 | FLORIDA

The Wake-Up. It was a late summer night in Florida. George sat on his screened porch, gazing at the stars. Flickering sparks of light danced above, a feast for the eyes. The pine trees reached upward, their tips seeming to comb through the stars like strands of tiny diamonds.

Then, something changed. A new vision appeared—not before his eyes, but within his mind. It simply *was*.

The first message was *Serenity.* Perhaps the word itself flickered briefly, but the feeling was undeniable. He was *in* Serenity—surrounded by it, infused with it. It radiated gentle safety and comfort. Being in this Serenity meant understanding it completely, because he *was* it, and it was him.

Next came *Love.* Not a word this time, but a pure knowing. He became part of something infinitely kind, tender, and accepting. It was sweetness without taste or shape—pure, boundless approval. Warm, embracing, uplifting, and yet humbly vast.

Then came *Wisdom.* He found himself in a realm of total knowing—of all things, their reasons, their origins. It was overwhelming, beyond the capacity of the senses. Like tasting the essence of every secret, every cause and effect, all at once. He silently pleaded, *Just a little more time here.* But then—it was gone. The vision never returned.

Not a day passes without George wondering what it was. Was he sober? Yes. Hallucinating? He doesn't believe so. The experience remains vivid in his mind. Others have shared moments like these. Some are afraid to speak of them, fearing they'll be dismissed as crazy, high, or unstable. Others call it a spiritual encounter—like Saul on the road to Damascus. Whatever it was, George knows this: it is something to be cherished forever. Hope springs eternal, and that truth endures.

His brother Ricky once whispered to him, *"It was a rainbow trout, not a brook trout."*

CHAPTER 07 | Italy

Pope Francis, born Jorge Mario Bergoglio in Buenos Aires to Italian immigrant parents, awoke in his chambers in the Vatican. He called out to his trusted attendant—no response.

Then a gentle, unfamiliar voice spoke in Italian:"Ciao, mio piccolo. Are you so proud now that you no longer remember your nonna?"

Startled, Francis turned and saw a luminous figure standing near his bed. The woman glowed with a soft blue light, her presence both calming and surreal. She resembled his beloved grandmother—his father's mother—Rosa Margherita. She had been his favorite, the one who had shared with him the old Piemontese poem, *"Aj Piemunteis ch'a travajo fora d'Italia,"* and taught him faith through quiet, loving strength.

"Grandma Rosa? Is that really you?" he asked.

"Si, è mia, bambino," she replied.

Francis reached out instinctively, arms open to embrace her. She remained still, her form insubstantial. He felt nothing but a soft breeze on his skin.

"I am from the spiritual place, Bambino," she said.

"I want to touch you," he whispered. "Don't you love me still?"

"Yes, deeply. I miss you, too."

"Is the spiritual place... heaven?"

"Yes, Jorge. It is something like that. I've come to share a message with you."

Her bluish glow deepened, pulsing gently like moonlight. "My guide and teacher allowed me to come. Many others wished to be the one to visit you, but those above chose me. They believed you would trust me."

"Oh, Gramma Rosa, I miss you so much. I still dream of our time together. You always inspired me."

She smiled softly. "Little Jorge—now Papa. My message is this: the wise ones who sent me believe it is time to help move life on Earth forward. The world is aching, and its nature needs healing. Fear, selfishness, and suffering are growing. But I know my good bambino—humble and kind—cares for the lost and forgotten."

"I'm listening, Gramma."

"We human spirits are still evolving. We long to grow closer to the Creator—and we are. But the fear and division between religions must be washed away. All souls come from the same divine source. No one religion holds the whole truth. Earth is one vast garden, even if its flowers are many."

Francis hesitated. "Are you saying... Jesus isn't the only true God?"

She answered gently, "Jorge, even I do not know all the mysteries. But I do know this: our Lord Jesus, on Earth, lived closer to the Creator than anyone I've known in this spiritual place. His wisdom and love are unmatched. Still, other faiths also hold sparks of truth. The Prophet of Islam was visited by a great spiritual being. The Buddhist and Hindu masters have guided many toward growth. And now, here I am—visiting you after death. What does that tell you?"

Francis bowed his head. "God of my understanding… it could mean I'm dreaming. Or perhaps I have a fever. But I feel awake. Gramma… are you teaching me again?"

She nodded. "Yes, my beautiful boy. The world needs healing. People must learn to let go of fear and selfishness. It's time to clean house—to prune the garden. Other teachers are already here or soon will be. They will find others like you—who can help guide humanity forward."

She said nothing of the darker forces also rising.

CHAPTER 08 | England

The nurse attending the frail man known to the world as the brilliant astrophysicist Stephen Hawking noticed a slight trembling around his lips. She had seen this before during his sleep, but today it was more intense.

"Are you having a bad dream, Professor?"

Stephen's eyes fluttered open. They looked distant—unfocused and full of fear.

"What is it, dear?" she asked gently, then added with growing concern, "I've never seen him like this before."

He appeared to be having a seizure—or perhaps something else. Alarmed, she grabbed the direct line to the on-call physician.

"Doctor, something's wrong. Please come immediately."

She had no way of knowing that Stephen was in the grip of a vivid vision—an encounter with his beloved, long-deceased mother, Isobel. Though fully aware she had passed years ago, the experience felt powerfully real.

"I must be dreaming," he told himself.

"No," his mother replied. "It's me. Your Mum. You're always surrounded by people, and I needed a quiet moment with you."

"But you died," he said. "And we both agreed—no God, no afterlife."

"Yet here I am. Real. Aware. And I know everything about you. I now believe I missed so much in my intellectual journey. There *is* a loving and powerful God—I see that clearly now."

"You're scaring me. Maybe this is just a nightmare."

"Stephen," she said softly, "I know this is hard for you. You're brilliant—especially in mathematics. But I'm here only to ask that you consider the possibility. That's all. Where I am, we share and learn and choose our next path. It's beautiful."

Stephen had long since learned that arguing with his mother was usually futile—she always won, and deep down, he never truly wanted to defy her.

"Well, Mother, I do miss you. And I've been feeling sorry for myself. This illness feels like a bloody prison."

"Oh, Stephen, how I've grieved for your suffering. Now, please wake up and have a nice breakfast. I love you—and my spiritual family just wants to know you're alright."

"I love you too. Can you come back and tell me more about this spirit world?"

"Don't worry. I'll be in touch." She glowed with a soft, white light. He felt a kiss on his cheek, a wave of warmth through his body—and then she was gone.

The doctor was suddenly in front of him.

"Stephen, wake up! He's coming around."

"Oh, thank goodness," the nurse breathed.

"Hello, doctor," Stephen said weakly. "Why are you here?"

"You gave us quite a scare," the doctor replied. "You seemed agitated—almost in a fit. How do you feel?"

"I'm sorry to alarm you. I had the strangest dream. Disturbing. Unlike anything I've ever experienced."

"Would you like to tell us about it?" the doctor asked.

"Maybe later. I just know I'm starving. I'd really like a proper breakfast."

"That's more like it," said the doctor with a smile. "Nurse, have the kitchen prepare whatever he wants."

"Yes, sir. Right away. So glad to have you back, Professor."

CHAPTER 09 | SPAIN

Life had gotten better. There was a workshop in Spain that taught George and others about trance and hypnotherapy. During deep trance one evening, the person George hypnotized began speaking in an old tongue. It was French—but not modern French. George, with his linguistic background, recognized it as an extremely ancient form of French, possibly from the late medieval or early modern period, with archaic syntax and words no longer in use. The woman was in her late 40s and a psychologist from Montreal.

"Please speak louder, Diane. Say it in English or Spanish." George asked her to switch languages because the old French was so obscure that even he could only understand parts of it. Spanish, being more commonly spoken in the region and by George himself, was a more accessible choice for both of them.

"Sí, cuando yo era una niña en Fuengirola, algo pasó."

"Tell me what happened."

"Yo tenía nueve años y jugaba con mi perro Josie cerca de la casa."

"So, you were playing with your dog near the house. What happened?"

The woman became visibly pale, and afraid. She began to sob. "Un hombre me tocó."

"You say a man touched you? How so? Tell me in English."

"He said his name was Asmodio, and he touched my hand. After that, I was in a place very dark, and it smelled like rotting meat. Asmodio pointed to my dog on the ground. Josie was dead. He told me he strangled little Josie and he was going to strangle me too. I remember trying to scream. He held me down and tore my dress off. He put his sex in me. I was in such terror and pain, and then I was in a different place. A nice woman like my Abuela held me. I think I died but was alive again."

George was shocked. It seemed best to raise Diane out of her trance. Asking her to slowly recall the building here and the group and the day. She became alert and focused in the present. She seemed calm and had a questioning look.

"How do you feel, Diane?"

"There is a horrible smell. Like a dead rat in the closet. I feel so sad. Like when my sister died." George asked if she remembered anything else.

"There was a dark place and a very bad smell. Then it was gone, and I was in a safe place and felt loved and cared for. No more smell either. My mind recalls soft blue light, clean air, fresh smells. A lady explained I was with her now and all was safe. We did not have bodies. Yet we were real. I understand it was the nest or home for our group. We were souls together."

"Can you tell me any more about what happened before you came to this safe place?" Diane showed fear in her eyes. She resisted going there.

"My guide told me how to handle this. She said other spirits in our group had been similarly harmed. My experience was one of the worst."

"When did this happen?"

"Is it alright if I call you George?"

"Sure," said George.

"It was around the year 1700. The town was a fishing village on the southern coast of Spain. I had a mother and a father, no siblings, and a dog named Josie. My father was a fisherman. My mother had a big garden." Without further hesitation, Diane said, "Now I remember. I was raped and murdered by an evil man, Asmodio."

"This is all so strange," said George.

"George, it is my understanding that my soul has been here before. I was damaged by someone or something evil. You know in my practice I work with girls and women who have been similarly traumatized. Being near the place it happened has brought this memory back."

"Yes, I remember that. Please tell me more about your soul group."

"The group has nurtured me back to spiritual health. Apparently, the man Asmodio was not just a man. There are disturbed spirits too. Maybe the word demon is not right. I am not convinced of that yet. Centuries ago, religious men and scholars of their day named them demons. Asmodeus was the name given to the demon of lust. Satan or Lucifer was the name given to the demon of wrath. The name Asmodio may have been coincidental."

George doubted that. "He sounds like a demon to me. Can we go outside, Diane? Let's see the sun and trees." They rose up and went to the terrace.

***

Outside, the evening was warm with a slight breeze from the sea. Shadows were long. The martins swirled overhead. They were playfully dancing in the orange light of sunset. They were designed for speed, sharp turns, marathon flights, and a high-protein diet. They ate bugs in the air. He never could actually see the bugs or verify the birds eating them on the wing. Little chirps sounded in the night air.

"How are you, Diane?" They found chairs out on the terrace. Lights were reflecting around the harbor in the distance.

"Something is troubling me. There is a sense of déjà vu. Having been here before but not knowing what will happen next. Does my prior life experience mean anything to you?"

"It is at least unsettling to me." George continued, "My study of past lives, spiritual experiences, and the overlaps between our physical world and the spiritual realm give me pause to consider your life today. Your past life as a child in this area of Spain is very important. What concerns me is the obvious coincidence of the same little village just over the hill from here. Could it be a slip that Fuengirola is common to this place here and your past life? And how has our workshop just come to be here now? I want to talk with our host, Dr. Swisher, and get his view on it."

Dr. Swisher was from Wake Forest University in North Carolina. His work into spiritual healing at the medical school led him to find intriguing evidence. What he learned was prayer for the sick made a difference. More got better and faster than those without prayer to help them.

The host doctor met with George and Diane on the terrace. After hearing the events of the day from Diane, he paused. "It reminds me of a workshop experience from last year. It was in Turkey near Istanbul. A woman revealed to her trainer and hypnotist, Dr. Greta Hilke, she had been murdered by an evil man in Malaga, Spain, around 1730. She may have more if Dr. Hilke has time to meet with us. Let me see if she can join us this evening."

Dr. Hilke was from Austria. A lovely woman, generous and wise. She had a private practice as a psychotherapist in Vienna. She was dressed in a white light cotton dress and wore open leather sandals. Her eyes were sharp blue, and her hair was drawn back in a dark fall. She spoke perfect English. Her smile was genuine and robust. After hearing Diane's review of the day, she said, "It is so much like Naomi's story. Naomi was my trainee in Istanbul last year. We kept in touch after the workshop. She revealed being the victim of rape and murder in her native town around 1730. It was Malaga, Spain.

She was supposed to be here this week. It seems she had to cancel. Her husband forwarded an email a few days ago. I tried to call her but got only a recorded message."

George said, "Dr. Hilke, during Diane's regression, she described the tragic events of her death in Fuengirola around 1700. She may want to share with you what she remembers."

Greta asked, "Do you sense anything evil about this event? I mean beyond just sick and violent?"

Diane spoke. "I am not convinced of true evil—not as some absolute force, at least. What happened to me was monstrous, yes. His name was Asmodio. He killed my dog. He raped me. He murdered me. I was nine years old."

A shadow passed over her face, but her voice remained steady.

"But evil? No. Evil implies something grand, almost mythical—a darkness beyond human comprehension. What he did was just... human cruelty, amplified by sickness and choice. My spirit group didn't just heal me; they helped me see that calling it 'evil' gives it too much power. It makes it something other, something unstoppable. But it wasn't. He was just a man. A broken, vile man—but still just a man."

She exhaled, her gaze firm. "That's why I help others now. Not because I believe in demons, but because I know monsters are made, not born. And if they can be made... they can be unmade."

Dr. Hilke spoke. "I am convinced there is true evil. With more experience now and Naomi's history, a pattern is revealed. Naomi reviewed the historical records of surrounding Malaga back to the year 1405. These records revealed the death of over one hundred girls around the age of ten, from 1405 to 1750. They were all sexually assaulted and strangled to death. Over the years in this area of Spain, public sightings were made of a disfigured man running away from the scene of the dead child. It also mentioned a horrible smell like foul, decayed flesh was around this man."

Diane whispered, "I know this smell. I have seen his yellow eyes. I pray to God to never see them again."

CHAPTER 10 | SPAIN

George returned to his hotel room feeling restless. He went out on the terrace overlooking the sea. The moon was luminous, nearly full. He recalled that those full moon nights were often horrific in the hospital while on call. Waves, like rings around a stone dropped in a smooth-as-glass pond, reflected their silent journey to the shore. He smelled the natural clean air and breathed in deeply. He considered all this talk about evil. He had accepted over the years that humans have a soul. Evidence now suggests that this soul can live on after it crosses the veil of death on earth. Near-death and past-life regression studies abundantly offered detailed reports confirming the afterlife. Was it scientifically possible? What a question. With humility and observation, a scientist found that quantum physics not only answers questions about the nature of light, it changes its answers based on whether it is observed or not. Suffice it to say, there is a lot of intelligence packed into DNA, and to believe that occurred only by random collisions over billions of years is not very intelligent.

A better question may be: Does every soul return to some spirit place after death? George did believe God to be generous. Even the wretched or tragically malformed or intellectually disabled or abused were important. So what about evil? Evil as more than just sick or ignorant or poorly raised? George learned, after growing up and practicing medicine, that the boogeyman was just a lot of fear and not understanding. Cause and effect—lack of something good does not mean bad.

He thought of himself as rational and always searching for the reason why things happen. He tried to keep his mind open and valued intuition. Evil does suggest a malevolent, hostile, destructive intention. Could it be a living being, as one can believe in a Supreme Being? Keep your mind open. If the Messiah recognized the devil, who was he to deny its existence? To himself, he said, "Enough of all this babbling. Go to bed."

CHAPTER 11 | SPAIN

That night, beneath the star-filled Andalusian sky, George drifted into sleep and began to dream. In the dream, his brother Rick appeared—healthy, strong, athletic, dressed in jeans and a football jersey. Smiling, Rick asked, "You want to go fishing?"

George stared at him. "Rick? Is that really you?"

"Yes, it's me," Rick replied. "Let's head north. I know a mountain stream up there with trout in it."

"But Rick, it's dark out. We're hundreds of miles south of there."

"Just follow me," Rick said. "Get up and put on some warmer clothes. It's cooler up north."

George got out of bed, pulled on long pants and a long-sleeved shirt. When he turned around, he was there—standing by a rushing mountain stream. The fading twilight revealed clear water gurgling over white and brown stones near the shore, deep and fast-moving at the center.

Rick handed him a spinning rod. "I know you always preferred this. I'll take the fly rod."

They cast their lines for a while but didn't get any bites.

"George," Rick said, "we're not going to catch anything right now. I want to tell you a story. Do you remember when we explored caves in the Ozarks?"

"Yeah, of course."

"I never told you this, but deep inside one of those caves, way back, I saw something. I didn't talk about it then because I was too shaken."

"What did you see?" George asked.

"It was… evil. I smelled it before I saw it. Then I noticed its yellow eyes glaring at me. There was a dead animal beside it—maybe a raccoon. I nearly screamed. It spoke first. It told me it would kill me someday, when the time was right. I was terrified. I ran as fast as I could."

"You're sure it wasn't just some creepy hermit?"

"No," Rick said. "When I was in the hospital recovering from brain surgery, it appeared next to my bed. It told me it hated me— for being good, strong, and handsome. Said it was jealous. That night, I died when a blood vessel burst in my wound. I bled out. My spirit group knows everything. My elder guide told me it was a twisted, evil demon named Asmodeus."

Rick paused, then looked at George intently. "I came to you tonight because I need your help. You and your friends at the hotel. He's hiding in a cave along the Camino de Santiago—El Camino. We're going to lay a trap. And then, we're going to kill the bastard."

CHAPTER 12 | SPAIN

George woke to the Mediterranean shimmering beneath him. Pink and green blooms came into view—oleander flowers, their scent attracting curious honeybees.

He sat up, the memory of a dream still fresh."Was it a dream? That was my brother. How could I not recognize him?"He remembered how Rick used to let him crawl under the covers when he was little—frightened by monsters or late-night horror films. Maybe Rick was scared too, though he never showed it.

George got cleaned up and made his way to the dining room, hoping to catch the others before they finished breakfast."Rise and shine," someone greeted. He grabbed some food and coffee, then sat down."I had a dream last night I'd like to share with you," he said.Greta nodded. "Let's hear it."

"My brother Rick came to me. He died over 40 years ago—he was 19, I was 16. He was special: strong, athletic, musical, and always ready to help those who weren't as brave. In the dream, we went fishing in Galicia. He told me plainly—he wants me to ask all of you to go with me to El Camino."

Diane tilted her head. "You mean the Santiago pilgrimage?""Yes, that's the one."

"I think this involves all of us," George continued. "Rick said an evil being named Asmodeus is living in a cave up there. He said he's going to kill it."

Diane gasped. "Oh my God." She began to tremble. "I can't go. I'm terrified of that thing."

Greta put an arm around her. "Listen—Naomi called me last night. She said a teenage girl entered her mind a few days ago. The girl showed her a hole in the ground in a remote mountain area. She's too scared to leave her home now. Her family farms livestock. She found signs of a missing sheep that had been attacked—blood and signs of struggle led her and her dog into the woods. The dog, known to be sharp and fearless, grew frightened near a cave and refused to go further. The girl ran home, and since then, she's been plagued by nightmares."

George's mind reeled. *How could this child enter Naomi's thoughts? How is that possible if they've never even met?*Tension grew among the group. Voices rose. Questions flew.

Dr. Swisher finally spoke. "I'm from the Smoky Mountains of North Carolina. Folks there lived far apart, but neighbors still looked out for one another. My grandparents used to say they'd 'get a notion' something wasn't right with someone—then they'd go check. It wasn't superstition. It was just caring for each other. But this... this talk of something evil does unsettle me. I've had enough of that fire-and-brimstone fear."

Greta offered a half-smile. "Then maybe we take your grandma's advice—go check on them."

The group nodded. It made sense. They agreed to head north, toward El Camino.

George thought of Rick again. *How can Rick be part of this, if he's gone from this world? Just a spirit in the sky?*

In the darkness of a mountain cave, two piercing yellow eyes gleamed.

CHAPTER 13 | IRAN

The Supreme Cleric of Iran, the Ayatollah, wondered if this day would ever end. He was tired from the squabbles of his political opponents. Kneeling in his chambers, prayer came gratefully. Allah was his only savior in this ceaseless struggle. He humbled himself to his merciful God.

"Ashadu an la ilaha ill Allah." There is none worthy of worship but the one true God. The Ayatollah is a holy man.

In his mind's eye, he sensed a glow of soft light. A voice in his native Farsi spoke to him, "You are my grandson after many grandsons. Peace and all blessings to you. I am Ibrahim. The same spirit that fathered Ishmael and Ishaq. My elder teachers of the spirit world have requested I share some words with you." The Ayatollah began to look around. "Who's there? Have I lost my mind? Has this troubled world brought me insanity?"

"Fear not, Hafeed. You are safe. I love you as your great, great grandfather. The life I live now is in the spiritual place."

"Are you in heaven, great grandfather?"

"Please be still and listen now, Hafeed. Can you believe that I am Ibrahim, also Abraham of your distant cousins?"

"Do you mean the Sunnis and the Ba'hai?"

"Yes, I mean them, and I mean the Jews too." The Ayatollah squirmed.

“Be still now. My spirit elders all want to assist you in your time of need. We want to help all Muslims and Jews to find forgiveness. We are all of the same Spirit. The earthly life has tested me and those before me. It can cause great sorrow and suffering. We are concerned for this time in the world. My word to you is to find a way to make peace with your fellow human spirits. One like me has gone to visit the Jewish people. We will not desert you. The time is now to find ways to build a future for your children and their children. All this anger and resentment will, in time, be replaced with a spirit of hope and friendship. We are, after all, one. One in our humanity and trying to grow towards our Creator.

“No one will believe me,” cried the Ayatollah. “I have preached death to the Jews and the Satan worshipers of the West.”

"Those far greater than I have sent me to you. Carry our love—for you and all of humanity—with courage and faith. The path ahead will require effort and time, but you will not walk it alone. We will stand beside you and others."

The prostrate form of the Ayatollah lay moaning in tears.

CHAPTER 14 | SPAIN

George had finished his coursework on past life regression in Malaga. He took a few moments to visit the terrace. The evening sun was melting into the sea. All was pastel orange, and the sea was gently reaching out to touch the shore. A tiny bird sat on the railing near him. Their eyes met for a second. Then the bird flew off to the rocky slope.

There is in Christian theology seven Cardinal Sins: pride, envy, wrath, sloth, greed, gluttony, and lust. George sensed the irony of their meaning. He did not necessarily accept them as true. What fun would life be without a bit of this or that? His studies said self-pride was the number one because it would separate man from God. George had seen cats behave with what appeared to be false pride. "I still like the little critters anyway," he thought.

The group was leaving in the morning for the north of Spain. The flight would land them in España Verde. The historic city of Santiago de Compostela was their rendezvous point. From there, they would travel east to the mountains where Naomi said the frightened girl lived. Diane finally agreed to come along but refused to enter any caves.

Santiago de Compostela Church. Galicia, Spain

George recalled case studies of people in deep trance speaking about what was important in reviewing their past lives on earth. The whole topic of past-life regression was considered unscientific and politically incorrect among most of the medical science community. The studies revealed that love and humor stood out as common themes in the dialogues. One needed to learn from the mistakes they made too. Little was mentioned about wealth, power, conquest, amazing discoveries, fame, or accomplishments. This seemed odd to George. Most of his life on earth had been predominantly devoted to obtaining knowledge for his work, helping sick people, finding a mate, having a family, wealth, status, and satisfying his instinctual needs. George wondered why the value of earthly pursuits was not mentioned more often by the more advanced spirits. What about the great music, literature, technical developments, and on and on? He realized none of this was possible without being alive on earth. Life seemed mostly a mystery. On an ordinary day, there may occur a thoroughly marvelous moment. He thought he may have misunderstood the message from the advanced spirits.

CHAPTER 15 | ISRAEL

Sara Netanyahu was sleeping in her bed alone. The Prime Minister, Benjamin Netanyahu, was away for a meeting with political leaders in Europe. She heard—or thought she heard—her name being called. It was three AM, and Sara was in a deep sleep. Half-asleep, she mumbled, "Who's there?"

"I am also called Sarah, and I want to speak to you."

Startled, she opened her eyes and sat up. "I said, who's there?"

"You know your Torah. I am the matriarch of the Jews. My husband was Abraham. Please wake up. This is important."

Frightened, Sara saw the outline of a lovely woman at her bedside. A faint glow of blue surrounded her body, and she wore a white gown. Her hair was black and long.

"Please calm yourself. We are very safe here. As I said, my name is Sarah too. I have been encouraged to speak directly with you by my elders. I am the spiritual being who once lived on earth, and my child Isaac was married to Rebekah. So began the long line of the Jews. You may have doubts I am who I say I am."

Sara was speechless. She touched her face. She looked around her room. There was a scent in the air—very clean and subtle. It was like spring air in a place she knew in the mountains of Italy. "God help me," she whispered.

"The elders say that is exactly why I am here. If you still doubt me, then touch my hand."

Sara reached out warily for the glowing hand. It was cool, soft, and reminded her instantly of the comfort she felt when holding her own mother's hand. So pleasant. All fear left her.

"Why are you here? What do you want?"

"All this suffering and death is needless. With your influence over your husband, the elders and I suggest that Israel pursue a peaceful and generous path toward resolving its conflicts with the Palestinian people and the Muslim world. My ancient husband, Abraham, has made a similar visit to the Iranian Cleric. The past must be reckoned with, and reparations made by all. Forgiveness can be achieved. Other spiritual beings will help along the way. It will require faith and hard work. This feud among fellow humans is wasteful—and it threatens civilization on earth. Gather all your resources and talents to convince the Prime Minister to take action, or else worse will follow."

Sarah squeezed the stunned woman's hand and then vanished.

Sara was bewildered, frightened, and unsure of her sanity. But her doubts faded as she recalled the touch of the spiritual matriarch. She got up and got moving.

CHAPTER 16 | SPAIN

George was in Santiago de Compostela in a hotel sitting room with his companions. George said, "A friend of the devil is a friend of mine." Diane nearly shrieked, "What are you saying?"

"It's just a verse from a Grateful Dead song. It was just playing in my head. I meant no harm." Diane was not smiling.

Greta had never heard the tune before. "I like it. In ancient Teutonic mythology, there existed dark gods of the forest. These were named and worn as images on their vests and armor before entering deadly battle. These mythical beings had fearsome power, brutality, and courage. The soldiers believed the dark gods would protect them during battle. Hitler and the Nazi SS tried to revive this practice. Evil is as evil does."

Dr. Swisher had studied the subject of evil for decades. He said, "Over the years, I worked with various scholars of philosophy and religion. Joseph Campbell studied the concept of evil. To summarize his findings, 'the more we know beyond good and evil, the more we can embody the good.' I think he is saying it takes experience and wisdom to understand what it is and what to do about it. Evil entities are not, in my experience, real. However, sick, disturbed, selfish, resentful, violent qualities are very evident." But there was doubt in his words.

"Dr. Swisher, will you take me back to a former life?" "Whatever for, George?" "Once before, in a trance journey, I perceived something in the corner of my eye. I think it was important and pertinent to what we are dealing with now. There may be a lesson to be learned here."

"Alright then. Let's go to the room."

Settled in the dimly lit hotel room in Santiago, George quickly regressed to the spirit memory of a life before. "Tell me what you see, George."

"There is someone with me. She is a bit more advanced than me. She is a spirit guide. We are in southern Spain, near the village of Fuengirola. I recall now that I was a sailor from a merchant vessel docked in the harbor. It was around the year 1450. I saw it happen while hiking in the rocky hills above the village."

"What did you see, George?"

"A wild-looking man is running with a young girl in his arms. She cannot be heard with the man's hand covering her mouth. They are below me on a path. He found a shaded place and pinned her down. I can see her eyes. She is like a young deer captured by a mountain lion. She is terrified. He tears her clothes off. He has his hands around her neck. He struggles to enter her virgin body. I want to scream out, but no sound comes out. My spirit friend calms me. It tells me we will get him soon. This is the past. It's little body lies contorted and lifeless. It is dead. Oh God!"

George is sobbing, groaning. Tears running down. Dr. Swisher says, "What is it? There is something else, George."

"Yes, as I ran toward the little girl, two men observed me. They were local villagers. They saw I was a stranger. They believed I was responsible for the rape and murder of this girl. Someone had shouted *"Socorro,"* and they just knew I was the one who had done this. I was restrained and taken to the jail. Neither my shipmates nor the captain could convince the angry mob I was innocent. The townspeople needed revenge. I was hanged the next day."

George was gently brought out of his trance. Dr. Swisher was concerned, worried. "How do you feel, George?" It appeared that George was actually calmer. "I understand now that this may explain why, in part at least, all my life I have accepted guilt though rationally it is not true." Dr. Swisher confirmed seeing this in others before. "Did you do it, George?"

"No, I did not."

"Good. Now let's move on."

Author at Santiago de Compostela Church

* * *

Before there was anything, there was grace. The spiritual principles of love, humility, integrity, kindness, faith, acceptance, forgiveness, and courage are all eternal. By grace, our Creator offered these to life. So dimensional time began. Experience has taught us wisdom. Beyond good and evil, there is understanding. Evil remains incomprehensible until one attains true wisdom—and such wisdom requires a depth of experience that often exceeds the span of a single human life.

CHAPTER 17 | FLASHBACK

When mother is unhappy, the whole family will suffer. George recalled the time Rick had a terrible seizure. Usually, Rick could rest for a day and his strength could be restored. This time, he lay in bed well past a day and still showed little spark in his eyes. George sat at his bedside. They were now both beyond their mid-teens. "How are you, Rick?" His eyes were blue-green, like a softer shade than their mother's. He was pale, empty, like a wet dishrag. His eyes were devoid of energy. "I am so tired. Why does mother hate me?" It surprised him to hear Rick say this. But he understood. "I think she must be sick," was all George could say. Rick said, "Our religion emphasized spiritual healing. I must be doing something wrong that my sickness gets worse."

"Rick, I pray for you every day. It's not fair. You suffer. I don't know about Mom. She still screams, and Dad tries to avoid it. I know this: You are a good brother. You do not deserve this. It is not your fault." Rick let out a weary sigh. His breath was sour. George touched Rick's hand and told him he would come by later.

Eventually, Rick decided to undergo surgery to remove the vascular lesion. After more than twelve hours on the operating table and the replacement of many liters of blood, the procedure was finally completed. George remembers praying with a desperation he had never felt. His father told him Rick was still unconscious.

The next day, his parents returned from the hospital. It was Friday the thirteenth, January 1967. His father looked at George and simply said, "He died." George collapsed into his father's arms, and together they wept with a grief deeper than they had ever known.

Later that evening, his father came and told George to apologize to his mother. "She thinks you blame her for his death." George found her in her bathroom. She was empty and cold. He said he was sorry and left. He didn't blame her, really. Maybe he blamed God.

CHAPTER 18 | SPAIN

They had decided to begin the journey on foot. Greta had spoken with Naomi by phone—she was at the farmhouse with the little girl. Naomi explained that the girl's father was Joaquin, a skilled hunter who planned to join them once they arrived. They would have horses and trained hunting dogs to assist.

It was May, and the mornings were brisk, nearly cold. Flowers and leaves had begun to bloom. The sun lifted above the eastern horizon. The group had eaten breakfast and was well equipped. The sky was clear, the air fresh with a stiff breeze. Rainfall was common in this part of Spain. Most pilgrims on the Way of St. James wouldn't arrive until later in the summer.

Their hike would take them eastward, away from Santiago de Compostela. No one carried a weapon, except Diane and Joaquin. She had a Swiss Army knife; he, a hunting rifle.

Dr. Swisher walked beside Dr. Hilke. "This area reminds me of home in North Carolina," she said. "Beautiful trees, lovely flowers in bloom. I can smell apple trees in the breeze."She paused, thinking back. "It also reminds me of my hikes in the Alps. I love the crisp air and the sound of birds overhead. My first husband and I honeymooned in the Austrian countryside. I miss Franz. He died only a few years after we married—microbiologist, taken by a virulent strain he was studying."

"I'm sorry for your loss," Hilke said. "Greta, what do you think we're here to accomplish?"

She hesitated. "I want to learn more about what Naomi has discovered. For the group, it's a practical extension of our classwork—and our professions."

"This focus on the man in the cave—potentially raping and murdering girls—that's beyond my call of duty. That's a legal or forensic matter. It's dangerous too. There've been several reports of missing hikers in this area over the years."

Greta nodded. "I respect your concern. If our work crosses the line from inquiry into danger, we need to back off. Call the Guardia Civil if necessary. Prisons all over the world are filled with murderers and rapists. In my experience, people have a choice. But sociopaths—they lack empathy. They can be clever and charming, but they'll do whatever it takes to get what they want. Often, they're intelligent and enjoy the thrill of getting away with it. When someone murders for pleasure or out of paranoia, that's not just a lack of conscience. That's evil."

"You may be right. From what I've seen, some of these people feel proud of what they've done. The act boosts their self-worth. History has shown how deadly sociopathic dictators can be."

"You speak with sound judgment," she said. "I don't believe evil can be trained out of someone's mind. Sensitivity training—hah!"

As they approached their first campsite, the weather held. They agreed to sleep beneath the stars. Someone lit a small campfire. Public facilities provided water and latrines. A small shop along the trail had supplied meats and salad.

Diane felt calmer, safe. She enjoyed walking the trail with George. She wanted to know more about him. Was he still married? Did he have children? Diane was alone after a loveless marriage. Her ex-husband, a lawyer, had run off with a client. Though often lonely, she was happier now. She had no children.

George lay back on his bedroll. The sun had set. The air was cool, crisp, clean. Diane sat nearby.

"How are you doing?" he asked.

"My feet hurt," she replied with a smile, "but otherwise, I feel refreshed. That little shower was perfect—cool, just right. How about you?"

"No complaints. No phone, no patients, no pets. That shower felt great—spring water, I think. I could smell the earth in it. I feel good."

"Any more mind-messages from your brother?"

"Not a word. Like he's gone now. Or maybe I imagined it. But I know better. When Rick made up his mind, there was no mistaking it. He was unstoppable."

Diane drew her knees to her chest and wrapped her arms around them. "I remember now what unsettled me about this journey. That fear is back. Those yellow eyes are still out there. Can we change the subject?"

"Of course."

"You said your wife was Spanish? Sorry if that's too personal."

"We're separated now. She's from Andalusia—southern Spain. It's a land of traditions: olives, fruit trees, strawberries, rolling orchards, the Costa de La Luz. She still lives near her family."

"What happened between you? You don't have to talk about it, of course. I can be nosy."

"Maria is my wife and a good friend for several years. Maybe we're still friends. We met when we were both lonely. Over time, we wanted different things. One tried to hold on, the other needed to grow. We drifted apart. My memories of her are okay—bittersweet, maybe. Couples either grow together or grind it out. Time tells who finds happiness elsewhere."

Diane nodded. "Some find what they need. Some grow in love. And some... just suffer, together or alone. My husband had a strong personality. He loved to argue—a trial lawyer. I admired that strength. We had some beautiful moments. But we lost our only child. She'd just turned six. Energetic and beautiful. We were in Canada, early spring. She tried to cross a frozen pond—stubborn as ever. The ice gave way halfway across. Her friend ran for help, but... she was under too long. Over ten minutes. I'll never get over it."Tears rolled down her flushed cheeks.

Lights out. Sleep settled over the group. George whispered a quiet prayer of thanks before closing his eyes. He remembered the day: the colors of spring, the crisp wind, the scent of new flowers.

He didn't know something was moving around the camp. A sniffing little varmint—a pest. Black eyes, sharp fangs. It found what it sought and crept off into the forest.

Rick saw it. He watched the little spy. He knew its purpose. It had picked up the group's scent. Yellow-eyes was using the animal to track them. Asmodeus would feed on the scent—especially Diane's. Her scent clung to her clothing, intimate and lingering. There was still a trace of the spirit damaged by his crime, centuries ago.

Yellow-eyes scooped the little spy into his arms. It whimpered. The cave reeked of death. Fog-like, heavy. Asmodeus stroked the creature's fur, then turned and scampered back to his lair. Lust stirred within him for what was to come. He cackled and drooled.

Rick saw it all in his spirit. No need for sneaking. The Elders had given him power—to see. Rick was a contact man now. He longed to grasp the putrid body of Asmodeus, to crush his skull with his fists, to strangle the life from him until all that remained was a rotten, ragged corpse.

CHAPTER 19 | SPAIN

Naomi was of Romanian heritage. She is a hypno-therapist in Bucharest. She has studied with Dr. Hilke in Istanbul. During the workshop, she became aware of her own past-life experience. She realized that being the victim of rape and murder as a child in Malaga around 1730 had a link to what was going on today. She met with the family in Galicia several days ago. The parents were humble people of this rugged land. Their only child was named Esperanza. For generations, people of Ireland had migrated to Galicia. The strawberry hair, blue eyes, and light skin were handed down to the mother and daughter from their Celtic heritage.

Naomi was able to gain the family's trust when she mentioned minute details of Esperanza's frightening tale. The family welcomed the appearance of this foreign lady who could calm the girl and offer comfort. Playing games in the home together allowed the girl to trust this woman. Her terror of the events around the cave diminished. Naomi told her some of what had happened to her as well. Not much of the actual violent outcome or the date it occurred—just enough so little Esperanza felt she was not alone.

The father had now devised a plan to protect his child and home, determined to free them all from their fear. He had friends to lend him horses and hunting dogs to seek out and track down this thing in the forest.

Joaquin had hunted for many years. His sheep and cattle were potential targets of the lynx and fox native to the region. He had weapons for hunting and was a good shot. In his experience, he had never encountered an animal like the one his child described with her frightened cries. Something she said about yellow eyes and the smell of rotting meat. Was it a human or marauding wildcat?

The local people would gather in church or at a fiesta. There had been stories of strange sounds and smells when others were in the forest. The priest, Padre Rafael, mentioned his own concerns for the safety of his people.

The Guardia Civil had questioned some of them about missing persons from the pilgrim trail. His hunting partner and friend, Pedro, trained the dogs. He offered to help search for this mysterious menace.

Diane stretched and inhaled the fresh morning air. She saw George still asleep next to her. The others were awake, moving about. She smelled the coffee and heard a bird chirping nearby. She got to her knees and saw what appeared to be scratches on the ground. Her clothing bag was open. What could have made these marks on the ground? "George, are you awake?" He moved and mumbled. "George did you see or hear anything last night?"

"What's that? What's going on?"

"There are fresh tracks on the ground around us. Some animal was here."

He got up. He looked at the ground.

"Yes, I see them. I didn't hear anything. Did you?"

"No, I didn't. My night was a blackout. I was exhausted and slept like a stone."

Dr. Swisher said good morning and offered them both coffee. Neither he nor Greta noticed anything last night.

Dr. Swisher said, "These tracks look like it was a pole cat or a badger was sniffing around the camp."

Diane felt uneasy again.

CHAPTER 20 | IRAN

The Ayatollah finished his morning prayers, ate breakfast, and scanned the day's schedule. Yet the vision from the night before would not let go. He tried to dismiss it as a mere dream, but peace eluded him. "Allah, deliver me from this pestilence—this evil dream. It must be nothing more," he muttered.

His life's purpose, as he saw it, was to spread his version of Islam across the world. That mission, in his mind, required the destruction of the Jews and the rejection of Western corruption. "The Qur'an demands that unbelievers accept the true faith," he told himself. "I will not be deceived by some twisted devil-dream. I will remain steadfast to Allah's will."

His anger swelled into rage. He would fortify his inner circle with loyalists. The liberal opposition would have to be converted, restrained, or cast aside. Support for jihad would be strengthened. New plans to strike the Jews would be drafted; larger attacks on the West would follow. Allah would grant victory. As supreme military commander, the Ayatollah had already spent more than eight months refining a secret plan. Two nuclear bombs had been acquired from a former Russian submarine base near the Arctic Circle. While the world pressured Iran into a nuclear treaty—and while his negotiators crafted a superficial list of concessions—his real attack plan neared completion. "The Prophet taught us to use diversions to mislead the enemy," he thought. "I will see the Jews scorched from the earth before Allah calls me home. My timetable is firm and without falsehood."

***

Abraham's mentor, known among her spirit family as Luiza, embodied a deep maternal love—though she had also lived as a man in other lives. Power, she believed, was sometimes necessary when selfish humans tried to impose their will. She had wielded it before in situations much like the one she now observed with the Ayatollah.

"Abraham," she said gently, "even a holy man can be blinded by self-interest. It is rare for those in their ivory towers to use power for God's true purposes. Clinging to worn-out, repressive creeds does no one good. The lesson has repeated itself again and again. The Ayatollah believes he's following Allah's will, but really he's echoing distorted ideas handed down by clerics who never evolved. I can't judge him too harshly—that's how people learn across generations. I, too, have been immature and confused. But the stakes are too high now. Civilization needs our help. He would do well to relax, to be humble and teachable."

Abraham listened quietly, turning inward. Part of him wanted to confront the Imam aggressively; another part loved him and wished him spiritual success. The tension tore at him. "It's time to visit him again," he decided. "Yes," Luiza agreed. "A squeaky wheel gets the grease."

CHAPTER 21 | ENGLAND

Stephen Hawking finished the meal. Well, the feeding tube had stopped delivering the blended eggs, sausage, and toast. He began searching his library of digital knowledge. "Let's see, spiritual beings: the nonmaterial essence of a living being. Sounds like a form of energy. If spirits exist, maybe I can find out what they are made of and how they move around. What a bloody crock. Mum, please come back and help me out here." And she did. She came to him in his dream again.

"So tell me, Mum, more about this spirit stuff."

"I will try. What it is cannot be defined by matter as you know it. Energy is a good start. It is alive, acquires experience, and grows. It is real. The living begins as the Creator's expression of grace. Beyond this, I am not evolved enough to say. I am still learning. I enjoy music. I write poetry. I love you. My curious mind seeks meaning. At times, I can be generous. Being with other spirits is like food for my soul. A soul is a tiny bit of God."

"So there are lots of souls? Even in other galaxies?"

"Oh my, yes! Spirits move around and are not confined by our material universe."

"I want to search for signs of life in other parts of our galaxy. It is a project I have just begun. Do you think we will find signs of life there with our radio telescopes and satellites?"

"The chances are excellent," she said.

Stephen said, "Thanks, Mum."

CHAPTER 22 | SPAIN

Stream Along El Camino in Northern Spain.

George continued his pilgrimage journey on the Camino with Diane. She was familiar to him in some intuitive way. Had there been a previous time they met before the workshop? "Diane, I wonder if we have met before. I get this déjà vu feeling about you." She said, "I wonder about that too. Like a distant memory. I honestly just can't say." They agreed to give it more time and let it unfold if there was really anything to these vague sensations.

"Tell me more about your life as a boy, George. I don't mean that Boy George. You know what I mean."

"I was a pretty happy kid. Always moving, running, playing sports. I never had a sister but a number of girlfriends. There was one special puppy love. Her name was Mandy. We were in grade school together. Her face, the freckles, her eyes, the smile— everything about her was like magic. I got up my courage one day in the park. I wanted to hold her hand. She let me for a while. We were just too young. I wanted to kiss her. She ran off then. Her mother was calling."

"So what happened?"

"Years later, I was watching a high school basketball game. I was attending a different school then since our family had moved. It was against my old school. She was in the crowd from her school. She was sitting alone. She was more grown up. Beautiful to me. I said hello to her. She remembered me, and we spoke briefly. A couple of years later, while home from college during summer break, I decided to call her. She agreed to see me at her home. We spoke and looked at school photo albums. I was very shy then. I asked her out but did not have confidence. She was busy making commercials for TV. We did not date. One evening, a few years later, I saw the Miss USA pageant on television. She won the whole thing. What a surprise. I never tried to see her again."

"Do you still think about her?"

"Rarely. It is odd that I even brought it up to you."

"What about your childhood, Diane?"

"I was a happy child. My parents were good to us. I have a younger brother who lives in Ottawa with his family. He is a corporate businessman. He travels a lot marketing the machines the company produces. We are not close. I am closest to my mother. She has been a source of support and kindness forever. She has helped me to go on after the death of my daughter.

I had a puppy love too. His name was Paul. It was around first grade. He was a fast runner and a really shy boy. The other boys respected him for his athletic skills. He liked me too. We did hold hands in the park. There were forests to explore. We ran along a trail and threw stones in the river. He did kiss me then. It was just fine by me. As time went on, we even used to play games. I was the nurse and he was the patient. I told him to remove his shirt and pants (giggling). I was only about nine, so we were not aware what we were doing. Then he became the doctor, and I was the patient. He wanted me to take off all my clothes. I was afraid and stopped with my underwear still on."

"Ha! Ha! I was hoping it got better. He wanted to see you in the buff."

"I did turn around and pulled my panties down enough to show my butt. That was it. I put all my clothes back on after that."

He touched Diane's hand. They looked into each other's eyes. She had big blue eyes with a gentle, open gaze. They were dark blue with wide pupils. Blue without blemish. George felt a wave in his heart—a moving, slow, and strong one. The tide was being pulled. "Whoa!," he said.

"You okay, George?"

"Ah, I guess so." Their hands released. Back on the trail again.

Up ahead, Dr. Swisher was heard saying, "There is a rest area very close to here. We can stop and sit in the shade. One more night in camp, and we will reach the farm this time tomorrow."

The group had made camp after a tiring march the second day. The air was dry and warm. There was still at least an hour before puesto del sol or sunset. Dr. Hilke could see a stream off in the distance. She needed to soak her tired muscles in the water. She informed the group of her intentions and set off without delay, weary and irritable. Her childhood in Vienna was not always easy. Her father was a successful businessman. Her mother was from a wealthy family and generally a good parent. She had two younger brothers.

Not often, but on rare nights, her father would come home drunk after a local meeting of the Teutonic Knights Club. The men spoke of politics and business problems. And they drank a lot. On one night, her father came home full of bravado and booze. His wife was usually upset with this behavior and rejected any of his advances. He decided to go into Greta's bedroom and kiss her and give her a hug goodnight. He decided to stay with her a little longer and sat on the bed beside her. Greta was just 10 years old. She was terrified of him when he got drunk. He began to touch her more intimately this night. He fondled her and then left the room. He never did have intercourse with her over the two-year period he molested her. Greta did not tell anyone. She was afraid to say anything to her mother. Once her menses began, her father no longer came around. She recalled these memories when she came upon the sparkling little stream. The invisible scars of the abuse were still there.

She found a swirling pool of clear water. The area was surrounded by blooming, flowery bushes. She sat on a flat gray stone in the water. Just a few moments of peace. She heard the water rushing by and then a bird calling its mate. "Franz, how I miss you." He had been the only man she loved. Their time together was too short. She believed she would see him again in the spirit world.

Greta removed her sweaty clothes. She put her tired body in the cool water. "AAAHHH!" The waters flowed from the distant Pyrenees. She washed her face and hair. She felt the chill of flowing sweet water on her face and then her entire body. Is somebody watching? Her senses sharpened and became more alert. "What was that sound?" She prayed when her fear came around.

She saw nothing around her. Reaching the shore, she pulled her clothes into the water to wash them. Then she smelled it. It was like a dead rat down in the basement. Something covered her face and pulled her violently out of the water. She screamed, but only a muffled shriek came out. The arms clamped around her. It was brutally strong. It ran with her into the forest, her legs kicking out at only air. She felt something like nails dig into her flesh. "Fight. Fight." It was no use. The claw-like nails dug deeper. Its strength was too great.

Diane thought about Greta. It was almost dark. "Has anyone seen Greta?" There was hesitation, and then George and Dr. Swisher began to look around. "She told me she would be at the stream to wash up and then be back in just twenty minutes." Dr. Swisher began yelling, "Greta! Greta! Come on, we've got to find her. All of us together." They got up and headed toward the creek.

Shadows were growing. Each was calling out for her, but there was no reply. The forest became silent except for them. They scrambled over rocks as they got closer to the stream. There was no breeze and no birds chattering. "Greta!"

"Over here," yelled Dr. Swisher. "Her clothes are here and all wet. Maybe she walked off a ways." Empty hoping. It became harder to see as the dark approached. They spread out to no avail. Their search gave up no further clues.

Diane said, "I'm calling Naomi. We need help. Let's see if I can reach her. We should have the police and some dogs here to track her down."

The call went through, and Naomi answered. "Wait and talk to Joaquín." He said, "Sí, ¿qué pasó?" Diane explained the situation. "Madre mía. We are coming now. Tengo mi amigo Pedro aquí con sus perros y caballos. ¡Vámonos!" Diane explained to the others they were coming with help.

Asmodeus was far away. He was in a new cave. Greta was lying on the rocky floor. She was not moving. Her eyes were closed. Her face was swollen from the knockout blows she received. Yellow-Eyes sat there waiting.

CHAPTER 23 | IRAN

The elder spirit was patiently describing the events on earth to the younger group. The elder was Luiza. In the group was Abraham, and behind him was the spirit of the previous Ayatollah of Iran. He had selected the present-day Ayatollah. Luiza used gentle, affectionate persuasion. She knew the spirit of the former Ayatollah was still new to this group. He was on the 'hot seat.'

Yet the other elders saw optimistically that this newer spirit was making progress. They all agreed that the earth needed a break. The reigning Imam of Iran would realize who was speaking to him when his former superior entered his chambers. There was hope that good would come of it. Luiza spoke.

"Given that the present acting Imam is planning to drop nuclear bombs soon, it is time to pull out our ace in the hole. You know the man you picked. Can you tell us—is he stupid or just stubborn?"

"Luiza, he is stubborn like a thirsty camel. I know how to approach him. Is it okay if I use a stick?" There was some chuckling now. "He needs to feel my words."

"I see," said Luiza. "Very well, do as best you can. Just a small stick then."

The acting supreme Imam was alone in his chambers. He was irritable and distressed over the final details of the secret plan. "It must work, and it will."

A shadow fell over his desk. "Oh no! Not you again." He turned around to see his mentor and the former Ayatollah glaring at him. "As Allah is great, is it really you, or is my mind infected again? I thought it was that Abraham again."

"Salaam Alaykum. Peace be with you. It is I, your friend and mentor." He held a long, gnarly stick as he spoke. "Yes, your mind is infected again, and my elder friend Abraham has spoken with me about you."

"What did he say?"

"He is a patient and devout spirit. He expressed his concerns for all the people you may harm."

"But—"

Whack! was the sound the stick made on the desk.

"Please listen! I have learned that my selfish old beliefs were wrong. All humans are spirits from the same Creator, and He loves us all. I was wrong to think others were infidels and to be destroyed. That includes even the Jews. I am learning to humble myself before Allah and my spiritual teachers. Much of Islam is good. The tired old ancient beliefs must go. Are you listening?"

"Yes, master."

"It is suggested that these secret bombs and terror plans be discarded. This is why I am here now. Please do this and pray to Allah for His loving forgiveness. The peace of our beloved Iran will be possible through our commitment to finding peaceful solutions. Salaam Alaykum." And then he was gone.

The acting Imam of Iran slumped over his desk and began to sob.

CHAPTER 24 | ITALY

This night, Pope Francis was disturbed. There was a dream enveloping him. It was terrifying him. There were two yellow eyes staring at him. The stench was causing him to retch. He woke up screaming. "Oh Lord Jesus, protect me!" Never had the Papa known such a terrifying moment.

There was a rustle of the sheets, then a glow of soft blue. "You saw him, did you not?" It was Grandma Rosa. The Papa was sobbing. His chest heaved. Tears were falling. Rosa spoke gently, "Pray and hold your faith, my good boy. You are safe now. The Holy Spirit will protect all of us from the evil. The evil one may be the same I once saw in Italy before you were born—yellow flaming eyes, brilliant and so full of malice. Jesus, Lord, protect us! It chased me on a hillside when I was just a little girl. It roared with laughter as I ran screaming in terror. My priest told me it could be one of the evil demons. I believe it was."

"Grandma Rosa, I never knew this. It was just as you say. It wanted to destroy me in the dream." He began to gather himself. "Why are you here, Grandma?"

"Yes, my lovely boy. There is a reason. My elders have asked that I deliver a message to you. This beast still lives here on earth. It is Asmodeus, the demon of lust. The elders want you to select some people of experience to help cast this foul thing out of life on earth."

Greta stirred upon the cold, hard stones of the cave. Her mind was a blur. There was pain in her head, and jagged stones jabbed her back. The dead smell was still there. She began to remember.

Yellow-eyes said, "So the human she-pig lives. Where is your protection?"

Greta said, "Who are you?"

Asmodeus rose and took a goatskin bag of water and tossed it to her. "Drink and wash off your face. I am going to have you now."

Oddly, she was not afraid. Some untapped courage was there for her. She said, "You smell like spoiled meat and behave like a spoiled child."

Asmodeus roared with animal anger. His eyes flashed a piercing golden rage. "Stupid bitch. Now you will understand."

He slapped her, pushed her backward, then placed her nipple in his mouth. He sucked for a few moments and licked her until it hardened. He bit down on it, and she screamed. Some blood was oozing. His penis was big and engorged. His stench overwhelmed her senses. He stuck his face in her crotch and licked and slobbered. He forced his tongue inside her. She gasped. He licked her like a thirsty dog. She groaned. His flicking tongue whipped around her crotch.

"More later. Eat bread. Drink water. I will touch you as never before and never again."

CHAPTER 25 | SPAIN

The men had arrived. Naomi was there too. Sunrise had begun. The horses were nervous. The dogs were squealing for the hunt. No time to lose. Find the trail. The humans could almost smell the scent. George spoke to Dr. Swisher.

"Greta is the only woman here who has not experienced what the others have already known. The Beast may want fresh meat. Ah, sorry, ladies."

"That may be true. He has her now. Let's find them." The scent was all around, and the hounds needed no coaxing. Joaquin yelled, "¡Vámonos!" The hunt began. Firearms were loaded and the safety was off. The lead dog was a powerful, full-chested male named Lobo. Intelligent, fast, and brave. Every dog and human knew he was in charge. He was a short-haired part Rhodesian and part Mastiff. Speed and power. A born leader. Yellow-eyes sensed they were coming. "Let them come."

George was riding an Andalusian gray horse. His name was Valo. Pedro told him it meant courage. Not afraid to enter the hunt or fight. Fast and sure-footed. George sensed he was not alone. His brother was somewhere watching. This was a chance for Rick and maybe George to reclaim some of the dignity lost by a shortened life. Pedro had given him a pistol and hunting knife. He gazed at Diane and found comfort in her game attitude. She had a score to settle. She rode with her black hair flying. Her horse was an Arabian black mare. Naomi was obviously an experienced rider. She was as one on the white stallion she rode, her head and arms forward, the horse's nostrils flaring.

Up ahead ran Lobo in the lead. The terrain was mostly brush and rolling hills. Some pine trees grew scattered all about. The hounds were yelping their excitement for the hunt. Behind them were Pedro and Joaquin, talking to the dogs, encouraging them. Pedro was the master and felt some concern for what he may have gotten his animals into. Any money from the extranjeros could not replace his precious dogs. Pedro took some comfort in knowing Lobo was in the lead. He was a wise and experienced hunter. The pack was slowing up ahead.

The riders gradually slowed their mounts. The dogs were in a frenzy. There was confused yelping and barking—all except Lobo. He was stopped and just standing on all fours, waiting. He was focusing on the brushy, rock-strewn hill. His nose quivered. He inhaled and raised his head. Pedro came forward and softly said, "¿Qué tienes? ¿Qué puedes ver?" Joaquin had seen this before on previous hunts. Lobo was calculating what all his senses were telling him.

Joaquin told Dr. Swisher to wait, and the others held back. The hounds were whimpering. They were wired for the hunt. One male tried to move past Lobo and was instantly rebuked with a snap on the rear. The younger dog submitted and retreated, tail between legs.

Pedro said, "Lobo rastrear solo. Es su manera. Esperen, por favor." George told them what was said and to wait. The other dogs were fidgeting about. The horses stood quiet and alert. Lobo moved up the hill and sniffed the air. Quickly now, he slipped away and out of sight. In a few minutes, he returned and went up to his master.

Pedro dismounted and knelt down next to Lobo. He was whispering to Lobo and then listening. Lobo circled around, then sat. Pedro said, "There is something there, but it is not the woman or the Beast. We must go see it for ourselves." George had translated this as best he could. Joaquin told the group to proceed slowly and follow his lead. The horses were reluctant and ill at ease. They went forward.

Valo proceeded with a nudge from George. His nostrils flared, and his head rose up, brown eyes bulging. Lobo stopped at the foot of the hill. Some tried to cover their noses. The stench of death. On the ground was the carcass of what appeared to be a boy. He was nude and desiccated. Maybe a few days. Pedro said, "I know this boy. His family is from the village near mine. This is the boy that has been missing. His name is Vicente. Ten or eleven years old." His face was broken and distorted. The eyes were open in a fuzzy haze of anguish. "My God, what could have done this?" said Dr. Swisher. The dogs approached slowly. Their heads were down as they sniffed. They drifted away, stiff-legged. The body was partially eaten around its belly and upper legs. Something scratched around in the brush. George saw a badger run off into the woods. Pedro asked, "¿Qué es eso?" George said it is a badger, and then the dogs ran after it barking. Joaquin dismounted and approached the body. He covered his face and made the sign of the cross. He used gloves and turned the body over. There were dried dark stains around the buttocks. It appeared to be blood. "I will call the Guardia Civil. I think the boy has been murdered." They moved upwind and made camp to await the authorities. George and Pedro continued on to find Greta.

CHAPTER 26 | ISRAEL

Prime Minister Netanyahu yelled, "Are you insane?" Sara could see the shock and anger in her husband's eyes. "You tell me the matriarch of the Jews came to you in a vision. What are you saying? This from my wife, a rational person that I trust above all others." She came close to him and touched his face. She hugged him. "Bibi, I am sorry this has disturbed you so much. I did not invite her. I am profoundly disturbed by all this too. I thought I was losing my mind." She held him closely, feeling his agitation.

He looked at her and said, "You have been a voice of love and wisdom for me. My joy and laughter. No, never once have I seen madness in you. Go slowly and tell me again what happened."

"She was here in this very room. She touched my hand. It calmed me like a mother would a child. Can you allow yourself a moment to be quiet and to realize we are still learning every day? Some things are odd or even surreal. Actually, for me, it is simpler this way. Spirits move on and continue to grow. The Torah says the same. I, for one, have never understood why our people must struggle to survive like a herd of antelopes. We are human too. And God help me when I say, so are the Muslims." Bibi fell into his chair by the bed, exhausted. He smiled a moment. "Will you come sit with me?" He took her hand and she sat on his lap. She rested her head on his shoulder. "Oh my Bibi." "Yes, yes, Sara. I love you, still. Even though you talk like some gypsy trying to frighten her neighbor. I am curious. Tell me more."

"There was a glow of blue around her. Her eyes were dark and her hair was black. She wore a white gown. I felt like I was with my grandmother. She suggested it is best that Israel find ways to peace with the Arab people. If we don't do it, all will become worse. Children will die or never be born. Find a way, she said. Other spiritual beings will help us."

"Never with a gun to my head. The Iranians are very near a nuclear bomb. They promise to destroy us."

Far off to the east, the Ayatollah had a meeting about the secret plan.

CHAPTER 27 | SPAIN

George knew he was just an amateur at horseback riding. Valo, his mount, was a powerful creature—graceful, fast, and generous with his rider.

Ahead, Lobo worked his way along the trail, searching. When he caught the scent, Pedro noticed immediately. "He has it," he said. Lobo no longer hesitated. He bolted forward, the other dogs following with sharp, excited yelps. Then, suddenly, the forest fell silent again. The high country was cool now, with a few hours of daylight still remaining.

Not long after, back on the trail, Lobo slowed and came to a halt. Pedro watched him closely. "He's thinking," he said. "Something's wrong. A disturbance." About a hundred meters ahead, large boulders and dense trees stood upon a rise. Lobo seemed focused on that place. There was no sound—not even birdsong.

Without a noise, Lobo took a wide path around the hill. "He checks the back door first," Pedro murmured.

The dogs followed. Pedro stopped his horse. Naomi, nearby, sensed it was time to wait again. Lobo circled the trees slowly and deliberately, finally returning to stop beneath Pedro's mount. The other dogs grew agitated, unsure how to read the moment. Lobo was beyond their instinctual understanding now.

"We'll approach the trees. Be ready," Pedro said.

They advanced slowly.

A piercing scream rang out—a woman's voice, high and terrified. It wasn't Greta's voice as George remembered it. It was a cry of pure fear. Lobo lunged forward at full speed.

"Ay, ay! Ahora. Ya!" Pedro shouted.

Valo reared back, nearly throwing George from the saddle. The dogs exploded into barking and howling.

Another scream came from the trees. Then George heard a brutal sound—something savage, likely Lobo. He had charged into the stand of trees, five dogs at his heels. What followed was an almost-human roar—deep and furious.

They all dismounted at the edge of the trees. Pedro approached the chaos with great caution.

"Foolish puppies, meet your new master!" he muttered grimly.

He saw a thick, powerfully built man—more beast than man— grab one of the dogs and hurl it against a boulder. The dog crumpled, its back broken. Another lay already dead.

Lobo, who had held back, now attacked. He lunged at the creature's exposed foot, teeth tearing into flesh. A furious roar followed. George arrived just in time to witness it.

The wild man was human enough to feel pain. He struck back, his massive fist connecting with the side of Lobo's head. The blow glanced off Lobo's left ear, but it was enough. Lobo lost his grip, staggered, then collapsed to the ground.

Pedro froze in horror as he saw his best dog fall. He raised his rifle and fired, but the shot went wide. Before he could fire again, the stump-like man dropped into a gaping hole in the ground and disappeared.

"¡Se acabó, lo dejamos, no más!" Pedro shouted. "Pull the dogs back. I'll take Lobo!"

George and Naomi moved quickly, helping to gather the remaining dogs. They retreated to the horses. Pedro cradled Lobo in his arms. The dog's head hung limp, but he was still breathing. Pedro laid him gently on a blanket in the shade.

George and Pedro returned to the site of the attack, retrieving the two dead dogs. They moved well away from the area—about 500 meters—and found shelter under a shaded grove. There, they dismounted.

"We'll wait here for the others," Pedro said.

Back in the dark cave, Yellow-eyes washed the blood from his foot with a rag. Smiling to himself, he gazed at Greta—unconscious and motionless on the floor.

CHAPTER 28 | ITALY

Some thousand miles away, Pope Francis had decided to take action. He spoke with Cardinal Vendici, and it was concluded to send experienced handlers of known cases of demonic presence. The cardinal had been in touch with some officials of the Catholic Church in Galicia. They confirmed the activities in a region near El Camino. The cardinal did not doubt the Pope when he told him about his visions and talks with his deceased grandmother. Cardinal Vendici had his own similar experiences. Pope Francis had heard of some Africans who came to Argentina years ago and were successful in disposing of a demonic presence there. They were Zulu people from South Africa. They had success in Africa too, in both Somalia and Kenya.

The Zulu men were courageous and powerful from their long heritage as fierce warriors. Their leader was the shaman Manqoba, whose name meant 'he who triumphs in hopeless situations.'. They agreed to go to Spain when asked directly by the Vatican. The local priest in Galicia was Padre Raphael. Upon receiving the call from the Papa, Padre Raphael was ecstatic. The Papa asked the priest to greet these warriors who were coming to rid the area of the cursed demon. Padre Raphael was very thankful and assured his Pope of every form of cooperation with the Zulu men. Padre Raphael could now tell his frightened community that help was on the way.

***

Luiza stood with her elder spirit group. The soft blue glow of the elders gradually deepened into a darker hue, becoming nearly uniform. Among the more mature spirits, gender was neither defined nor recognizable. Names were rarely used, and communication seldom relied on spoken words. Instead, intuitive and emotional expressions were transmitted simultaneously to the listener—they were, after all, telepathic.

Luiza noticed that the elder group had invited Rick to join them. It was somewhat unusual for a younger spirit to be included in an elder gathering. She greeted him, and he returned the greeting. His glow was a bright, light green.

One of the elders brightened and spoke. "Think of me as Joe. Some in the group have called me other names—like Meathead, Bozo, Dork, and worse. Anyway, we are a joyous bunch and have great affection for you, Luiza—and for you too, Rick. There's a pest troubling people along the El Camino in Spain. He's a very bad apple. My friend Fred here knows this asshole—his name is Asmodeus."

A blinking light grew brighter and said, "Just call me Fred. Yeah, I knew him even before he ended up in Spain. We were younger spirits together. He didn't like the way things were done—chose to go his own way. Huge ego. Selfish. Always blamed others for his suffering. But deep down, I think he was just afraid. He was strong and clever, but also abusive and cruel.

He never grew spiritually. Eventually, he found a renegade group, and I never saw him again. I know he's been raising hell on Earth for centuries—murdering, raping, ruling through fear, terrorizing those he captures. The group has asked me to accompany you and Rick on a mission to remove Asmodeus from the world. Rick, are you in?"

Rick's glow brightened. "Let's do it," he said.

Joe turned to Luiza. "Luiza, you're being asked to support the Zulu warriors. They may need backup. This isn't a game. Asmodeus is a tough nut. He still holds some spiritual power. Enough is enough. Get him the hell out of there."

CHAPTER 29 | SPAIN

Greta had the trousers, shirt, and shoes of some boy on. They were torn but fit perfectly. They afforded some warmth in the cave, and they smelled much better than her captor. She had been raped again. He did it in her rear the last time. She was bleeding from behind. He was insatiable. His vice-like hands were around her neck when he came. She went unconscious momentarily. He dropped her when he came, and that allowed her to breathe again. The pain was unbearable now. She would scream, and the stump-man loved that.

"Why are you doing this?" she asked.

"Because I want to and I can. I know of your spirit work. I know of your father molesting you. You have suffered. So have I. Once, hundreds of years ago, I was in a spirit group. There was an elder who visited us. I trusted the elder, even loved her. My life on the earth before I died was a torment. My mother was from an aristocratic family in Constantinople. She was raised Orthodox Christian but despised the cleric hypocrites in the church. She was often left alone by my father when he went away on business. She would entice me to her bed when I was about 12. She liked to arouse me and tell me how it excited her. She did everything but get pregnant with me. There was pleasure for me as well, I admit. She was still a young, lustful woman. She feared getting pregnant and sent me off to a prep school. The priest there knew I was confused in some way. He liked boys and began to have his sexual way with me.

I ran away. Being 15 and looking 18, the army took me. I was a victim, so you see?”

Greta said, “Yes, I see. How did that life end?”

“We had captured a village. I was on a rampage, looting and drunk with my fellow soldiers. They were Muslims that we had vanquished. I saw a young virgin in a home. She fought me and screamed, but finally, she surrendered. As I fucked her, her father came into the room. He had a club and beat me to death.”

Greta asked, “You mentioned someone in your spirit group you loved and respected. What happened?”

“The elder spirit. My spirit group was made up of mostly sexually abused people. It was rare for a boy to have been abused by his mother. I was the victim, though many did not understand me. The elder was also abused by his mother. He understood. But he kept saying I had to accept this as a painful lesson of why it is wrong for parents to abuse their children. Eventually, I left the group. I was not wrong and would rather punish others for what had happened to me. I resent all the elders and even God. There are other souls like me, and we refuse to accept a painful lesson for damage done to us. We are unique and have our own special path. Our power will conquer those that think they know the right way and are better than us.”

Greta could see her father’s eyes in her mind. He was touching her in her bed again.

"I can almost read your thoughts," he said. "You could join us. There is power among us. These self-righteous will learn about our power."

"I have known love. My husband gave it to me. I am sorry for the pain you have suffered. I try not to judge others. It is there for all of us if we can get past the hate and work to understand and then love again."

"For that, you will feel my power as I send you to your cowardly afterlife."

Asmodeus began to mount Greta again. A light of blue and green appeared in the cave. Fred and Rick were there now.

"Remember me?" Fred said. "You are the one who blamed everyone else for his terrible life. I brought a friend here with me. You may remember him."

Asmodeus backed away from Greta and said, "I am the master here. Stay there, wench. See my power as I deliver these losers back to where they came from."

Rick said, "Maybe you remember me from the hospital. You opened a vessel in my brain, and I died. You said you hated me for some reason. Why did you hate me?"

"I don't answer to you. Fuck off!" said yellow-eyes.

Fred stepped forward. "Listen, asshole, I stayed with my spirit group. We learned more than you may ever know. We are taught to protect ourselves and others if necessary." Fred was once a tough kid on the streets of Chicago. Some of that was still in his spirit.

Stump-man charged him with a roar of anger. Fred had a wooden bat in his hand behind his back. He stepped aside and whacked Asmodeus like a clean-up hitter right on the nose. It sounded like it had struck a rock.

Fred said, "Whoops, slipped." Then he drove the bat right into Asmodeus groin.

Asmodeus screamed. He grabbed his crotch with both hands. The bat came around one more time on top of the head. It sounded like a coconut was struck. Fred saw himself like Ernie Banks hitting a homerun out of the park.

"Hmmmh! That felt nice."

Yellow-eyes was out cold. Fred said to Rick, "I'm sorry for stepping in front of you. Next time, after some practice, it will be your shot."

"Ok, Fred. Nice move."

Fred asked Rick to take Greta out of the cave. Rick gave her some clothes and asked her if she could stand. She tried and stumbled. Rick picked her up and carried her out. Fred said he would be along shortly. Fred had the idea to finish the job for good.

Rick carried her all the way to the camp.

"Thank you for saving my life."

Rick told her she was a brave woman. Naomi and Diane came running over. He placed her on a blanket in the shade. They gently hugged Greta. Diane went for some water and clean towels.

George ran up to Rick and hugged him. "Oh Rick, how I've missed you."

"I am here for just a moment. Fred wants me back in the cave. He kicked ass on yellow-eyes. It is best I get back there now."

George said, "Who's Fred?"

But Rick was running like the wind through the trees. The sky was turning orange. George felt so grateful for having seen his lost brother again. His grief and anger were beginning to lift like a fog in the morning.

Rick ran like a zephyr to the cave. He entered and found Fred's body on the floor. His head was smashed in like a squashed pumpkin. Blood was all around his distorted face. A light of soft blue was above the body.

Rick heard Fred's voice in his mind. "He tricked me, Rick. He is a sneaky little shit. The elders won't be happy with this. He played possum with me and hit me on the head with a rock. Leave the body. It has no more use and will fade away. My guess is he has run off to some other lair. For now, come with me back to the spirit group."

They left the cave like dust in the wind.

Yellow-eyes wasn't smiling this time. He was very pissed off. Running now with a broken nose, a walnut-sized lump on his head, and balls that felt like two overripe tomatoes, he was making his way to his favorite cave further up the mountain.

Asmodeus

CHAPTER 30 | IRAN

The general entered the Ayatollah's chambers. "Peace be with you, General Saladeni." "And also with you." The general was a man of tradition. His devotion to the Imam came from a long family history of military Muslims. The family comprised generations of warrior patrons, totally committed to protecting and serving the Islamic clerics of Iran.

"Please be seated. Something has happened that has caused me to be emotionally perplexed." The Ayatollah closed his eyes and whispered a prayer, "Allah, please guide me. Your will is mine."

"I am listening with all my devotion to you. I trust your love of Allah, the one true God," said the general. The general saw the distress on the man's face.

"By Allah's will, I have had visions. I was visited by the spirit of Abraham and, most recently, my mentor, the Ayatollah before me. I question my own sanity. My faith in Allah remains true. All things are possible with the Creator. Do you think I am insane, General?"

"I trust what you say is true. You are a holy man."

"Thank you. I was told by my mentor that we must find better ways to solve our problems with the Jews and the Great Satan. He made it clear to me that if we try to destroy Israel and the evil West, all will get much worse for our people and the children yet to be born. I share this with the respect you and your family deserve. I am not insane. Though I am disturbed by these visions, I am convinced they are real. I accept my responsibility for the plan to drop those bombs. Now I must obey those who have more wisdom than I, as Allah wishes.”

The general was in shock. “Maybe he is going crazy,” he thought. He stared in disbelief.

“Please, General Saladeni, try not to look at me like I am a lunatic. My own reflection in the mirror troubles me enough. Please stand down the bombers. For the present, find a safe and undetectable place to hide away the nuclear bombs. They said they should never be used. I am following his words and ask you to obey me and him.”

The general’s eyes were black and shone clearly. His shoulders slumped as if to surrender. “I trust your words. I too believe Allah’s ways are best. The bombs will be placed in a deep underground mine. It is deserted, and they will be safe there until further notice. I will obey your orders now and when you give me further instructions. When they are safely placed in the mine, I will inform you.”

“Good, General. Salaam alaykum. As Allah wills.”

“It will take a few days, Holy One.”

And it was done. The bombs were safely deposited in the abandoned mine. The Imam was given the message. The problem was averted for the present.

CHAPTER 31 | UNITED STATES

One day, after prolonged drinking, George took a handful of medication and washed it down with a beer. He did not die. He awoke on the floor hours later, unsure how much time had passed. Remembering his desire to die, it seemed that the time had not come. A friend in the program took him to the hospital. It took weeks afterward to function even in the most basic way.

George attended meetings. He slowly revived. The group he went to believed there were other things he was meant to do. They said God expected more from him. George did not know what that was. He surrendered to the program. There was a God in his mind, and he prayed to this God. The obsession to drink had left him.

For years, gambling brought charm and pleasure when downtime was needed. Large stacks of cash were often received. Everyone loved a winner. The house took care of George—free everything.

Years later, George was to pick up his wife at the airport as she returned from Spain. With a few hours to wait, he decided to go to the casino. He lost all his money. Just as he left, his wife called him on his cell phone. She was not in Tampa as planned—she was delayed in Fort Lauderdale. She wanted him to pick her up there. "Oh shit." It was one a.m., no money, and a very angry woman was waiting.

It took four hours to drive across the Everglades. It was a starry, cool night in November. The car had been filled up before going to the casino. She had been up for 28 hours. She was mad as a wet hornet and did not yet know he had lost everything. There's truth in the saying about Spanish women having a hot temper. After running around the airport, he finally found her. Her eyes were mean. No hugging or kissing.

When George could not find change to pay a toll, he told her what had happened. Very rapid, machine-gun Spanish came out of her mouth. These were words he had never heard her say before. He didn't want to know their meaning.

About a week later, she decided to return to Spain. He made sure she got to the airport safely. The lease was up, and George wasn't sure what to do. He was homeless and chose to stay at the Salvation Army for a while. He continued to go to meetings.

He met a young man at one of the meetings whom he had seen before, sleeping in a park. He was a pilgrim for Jesus. He said, "You're trying to fill the hole in your soul." George did not want to be saved. No offense.

After about a month, a friend from the program said George could stay at his apartment until he figured things out. He went to a meeting every day. He began to feel better. Maria said she still loved him.

A few months later, George went to Spain to see his wife. It was late spring and already very hot in Andalusia. The sun shone like a blistering beacon. The Atlantic waters were cool and revived the spirit. The people were friendly and sociable.

CHAPTER 32 | SPAIN

Lobo rested his head in the lap of Pedro. His eyes were closed. "¿Cómo estás, Lobo? Tú vives, mi amigo. Gracias a Dios por eso." Lobo stirred and opened his eyes. Maybe he had a thought about yellow-eyes. He sighed.

The group was all together again. In addition, the Civil Guard and two local policemen were there. They were motivated. Word had spread that even the Pope was involved in the hunt for the wild man. Greta had seized their attention, their brows lifting in alarm as they tried to imagine what kind of monster this murderer might be.

Greta, now wrapped in a wool blanket, had been seen to by Dr. Swisher earlier. Her pulse was strong, but her body bore scratches and bruises. Swisher had cleaned the wounds, checked for concussion, and given her a mild sedative to help her sleep. She had drifted off beside the fire, finally safe after the ordeal. Naomi and Diane sat on either side of her, watching over her like quiet sentinels.

Father Raphael was in León to greet the Zulu warriors. He had called Joaquin to say they would join them the next day. He told Joaquin the Papa had asked the African men to assist. For Joaquin, an intelligent but simple man, this all seemed very strange. Demons, spirit doctors, the Papa, and now Zulu witch hunters. He missed his home and feared for his wife and child. "Dios mío, Jesús, José y María."

All were fed and now sitting around the campfire. The pine logs snapped and burned red-hot. Dr. Swisher and George were talking. Having seen Rick running with strength and seeing his blue-green eyes again, George was in a mood of joyous homecoming. He wondered what had happened to Rick after he disappeared back into the trees. The cave was found empty later.

* * *

The Zulu warriors stood like skyscrapers over Father Raphael. The priest welcomed them as they arrived in Leon. He reached up to shake their hands. Manqoba spoke English, and so did Father Raphael.

"Thank you for your personal welcome. My companions are named Msizi, Nomzamo, Thando, and Ulwazi. We are humbled that the Pope has asked us to come here. We will do our best."

"Our community here has been deeply troubled by this evil. We need peace and safety to return. Come with me to our van. We can talk more."

The cargo of the Zulus revealed odd shapes of covered tools or instruments, costumes, and clothing. The drive began. The priest made a short prayer of protection for the brave men. He asked that God grant them courage and strength to rid the land of the demon.

Manqoba began a prayer, and the four warriors chanted a deep, slow melody. The priest was curious as to how they performed an exorcism. Manqoba began:

"We are the people of nature. We know animal spirits and their manifestations. Nature has beauty, power, and many forms. At times, an evil spirit can enter an animal or man. We are not taught, nor do we understand where it comes from. Over eons of time, our people have learned to protect our animals, plants, and ourselves. We use our dance, rhythm, and time-tested medicines to talk to the necessary nature spirits. We humbly ask for their help. Nature knows what is needed."

A natural remedy, the priest mused. God created nature—perhaps this wasn't so strange after all. Who was he to question it? Hadn't Jesus Himself performed miraculous signs through natural elements? If the Zulus could summon the spirits of nature to confront this darkness, then perhaps that, too, was part of God's design.

Father Raphael's thoughts turned to the past—centuries marked by unspeakable cruelty, when evil was met with torture, burning flesh, and brutal dismemberment. Was such savagery ever truly necessary? In his heart, he believed it was not.

CHAPTER 33 | LUIZA

Luiza was present in spirit. She was only a few dimensions away. Not really a spy. More a covert consultant. Luiza had many human Earth lives, some of which gave her unique insight into 'yellow-eyes.' She knew of times past when outer evidence of demonic presence was misleading. During her last life on Earth, she was somewhat of a celebrity in her Amazonian Indian tribe. She had been lost during an attack by the pioneer Portuguese settlers. She was found and adopted by a kind woman of the colony. She was six when this happened.

The woman was from an educated aristocratic heritage. The woman was named Linda Luiza Valdez Bellem. She was a teacher and musically inclined. She gave Luiza her middle name, which was also her grandmother's first name. Little Luiza was accepted as a true family member. She was often teased and tormented by her siblings or the other children. But her mother was very protective. "Luiza, you are special. I love you and will guard over you like my grandmother did me. I will be here for you like that mother hen watches over her chicks. You are pretty and clever."

"Obrigado, Mama. The other children call me *indio* and jungle bird. They know you are never far from me, so they don't strike me. I have one good friend, Gabriella. So I am happy. My two cats also love me as I love them. They were lost in the jungle when I found them, just like you found me."

"I am proud of you, Luiza. Someday we will go to find your family in the jungle. Only if you want to, that is, *Dulcita.*"

"Yes, I miss them."

Some years later, they did. Luiza was 15 years old, a young lady now. She went with her mother and one of the men from the hacienda—a skilled hunter and very good with rifle. The year was 1754, in the time of Christ.

There was heaviness in Luiza's heart that day. She was dressed only in a simple white cotton cloth dress. For years, she had felt a deep, silent resentment toward these Portuguese expansionists. Her family had seemingly abandoned her in the forest. Her adopted mother had explained the circumstances. The love she held for Linda, her mother, partially saved her from a slow-burning bitterness. Yet she was confused that her own people had left her and never tried to rescue her. Could she find an understanding that might release her from this tangled web of emotions?

The nomadic tribe must have relocated recently. The hunter had led them to their last known village. What remained was little more than charred remains of the empty dwellings. Fresh mounds of dirt told of recent burials. The natives were gradually dying off from new disease outbreaks. It was thought the white settlers were responsible for bringing new plagues. The Indians had to move deeper and deeper into the forest to escape these torments.

The hunter guide, Manuel, decided to cautiously follow the trail left behind. Two more days and nights traveling over rivers and valleys, enduring bugs, snakes, lizards, and odd screams at night, they spotted a new village. The three trackers were ragged, bug-bitten, and exhausted. "Oh, for a clean bath, a hot meal, and a bug-free bed," said Señora Linda.

"Manuel, you have been a trusted guide and protector. We must gather ourselves now and wash away our sweat and fears. Let us wash in this little stream, clean our clothes, and eat some fruit. Then we can enter this village, Luiza."

Though fearful, Luiza was excited to see a family member or friend. "I have dreamed of this moment for years. Thank you both for your help."

***

Luiza wanted to go in alone. She feared the white people would frighten the natives and force them to attack. "I will enter alone. Please stay here."

"What if they try to harm or even kill you?" said Señora Linda.

"I must take that chance. Why would they try to hurt a girl who looks like them? Please, Mama. Let me do this."

"*Bueno*, Luiza, I do understand. We will wait here. Such courage you have. Maybe they will allow you safe passage. But after ten minutes, we will come after you, regardless."

Luiza hugged her mother and then Manuel.

***

"This is like a dream. I have walked into my family village a thousand times before."

As she approached, there was a stir, then shouting. Children ran to see what was happening. Then armed men with spears walked forward. One man with eyes like a hawk and long black hair came forward. He looked fierce and malevolent. Luiza stopped and knelt on the ground twenty feet from him. The warrior slowly walked forward with a stone axe in his hand. He raised it. There was hatred in his eyes. He thought of the deaths of his friends recently.

A young woman screamed. "Layla!" She ran forward, shouting in her native tongue, "Layla, Layla!" She knelt before Luiza. She was naked but for her loincloth. She looked at the trembling stranger. She lifted up Luiza's face with her hand. Their eyes met. A moment passed. All the natives were frozen in breathless curiosity. There was a stirring in the air, like some huge creature had given up its breath. A sigh. The Indian maiden had some light in her eyes. She was smiling. In her own tongue, she said, "My baby sister."

The villagers looked more closely. The warrior lowered his weapon. "She is my sister, Layla."

Luiza recognized her older sister now. Her eyes brightened. They hugged each other with tears of joy. Luiza said, "Didi, oh Didi."

The villagers were in disbelief, whispering and chattering. The natives gathered around the two weeping women. Others began to agree it was Layla. Didi took Luiza into a small shelter made of branches and leaves. An old man was there who listened to the amazing story of what occurred.

The native elder agreed to let the two white people enter the village. They were to be unarmed and not touch anyone or anything. Thus, Luiza had come home to her native people. Luiza began her life's work that day as a budding anthropologist and teacher to both worlds.

CHAPTER 34

She breathed in the jungle after a brief torrent—earthy and fresh, sweet flowers on the air, a soft breeze whispering. The jungle beckoned: *Come this way.*

It was approaching *vespertino*—shadows lengthened, silence settled, droplets fell on leaves. Not yet evening, but close.

Luiza followed the call. *Come this way*, it said again. A *loro* sang it too: *Luiza, come this way.* A low rumble echoed like distant thunder. The jungle exhaled the breath of life, ancient and maternal.

She parted a curtain of prehistoric palms—and saw it.

Blue, green, aquamarine. A shimmering veil, like a spectral hologram. A stream flowed with clear rainwater, light refracting in shifting rainbows.

She stepped in barefoot. Cool water swirled around her ankles. Spongy grass embraced her feet.

On the other side, a glowing, waving portal opened around her. It enfolded her—warm, still, peaceful. Like lime pie and *café con leche.*

She felt safe.

"Thank you for accepting my invitation," a voice said in her mind.

It was her mother. Her real mother.

"Mama?"

"Yes, *carinho*. It's me. Listen, and let me stay near. My spirit still lives. I wanted to tell you where I went. You were so young."

"I remember. Didi told me..."

"I was wounded in the attack on our village. My head was struck. I died a few days later. I couldn't find you before I passed."

"Mama... Can I touch you? I want to hold you."

"You can feel me. I'm spirit now. Can you sense me?"

"Yes... It's warm, like a soft blanket. It smells like you. Oh, Mama..."

Tears slid down Luiza's cheeks as she closed her eyes.

"The elder spirits made this moment possible," her mother said. "Now you know my soul lives. It misses you. And it is healing. Love has power, Layla. You'll need it one day—to face a darkness coming to this world."

And then, Luiza was alone again.

***

The shaman of the village was a wiry old man with one arm. He was called the cat-man because he fended off a vicious jaguar attack when he was ten years old. The Beast did make off with his left arm. Thereafter, he learned the ways of the jungle to survive and be useful to his people. He was not a capable hunter anymore, but he became a guide to those needing remedies.

The cat-man was a connoisseur of plant and animal potions for wounds, fevers, hunting, and spiritual rituals. Luiza observed how a potion of the Ayahuasca plant was consumed by a native. The result often made the person become focused on something or someone present but not visible to others. When Luiza asked about this, the man or woman said they were conversing with spiritual beings they knew. Sometimes it was spirits of people they once knew. At other times, the spirits were unknown or even of non-human origin. There were "dark spirits" that were encountered too. The native would become frightened or even terrified. Luiza listened to the accounts of the frightened natives and the horrific images these dark spirits could insert into the mind during these altered states of consciousness. Luiza never took the plant potion herself. She was afraid of it and preferred a clear mind to observe her surroundings. She chose to remain safe.

The cat-man invited Luiza to accompany him on his sojourns into the jungle. He collected portions of plants and roots for medicinal purposes. On such journeys, the shaman explained how to call forth the spirits inhabiting a region. The spirits might use an animal such as a bird or a plant such as a vine or tree as a platform for expression. Once introduced to a spirit, Luiza learned about their identities and their qualities. "Were there evil spirits?" The cat-man said yes, there were. He saw them as sick, angry, afraid, or without internal harmony. They could be managed or even destroyed by other spirits that were healthy and positive. Luiza found she could focus her mind's eye on a spirit and it would often come into her mind in conversation. She could ask for help or just communicate. "What are you doing today?" The response, "I am encouraging bees to visit these plants to spread their pollen."

She learned that a few bad spirits had failed to grow. They refused to get help and could not climb the ladder of life. These bad apples were eventually returned to a place of healing. If there was no progress, they might be dissolved into their essential energy. Luiza learned what signals could be sent to get help in dealing with these bad apples.

***

One day, the cat-man asked Luiza to follow him into the jungle. "It will be a two-day journey to reach this place. It is where the dark one lives. He is pure evil."

Luiza said, "I do not know what that is."

"The dark one will try to enter your mind as we come closer. It will use the jungle to romance you. Make use of what I have taught you to protect yourself. Some older spirit has told me in a dream to assist you. The spirit wants you to learn more. You are special and will need this experience for your preparation."

Along the way, Luiza crossed rushing streams. In a pool, vicious needle teeth surfaced for insects. A frog of green and yellow scampered on the shore, chased by a small cayman. It landed in the pool and was devoured by the needlefish. Birds of green and red and blue-like purple cooed and whistled. The old man pointed to a ledge hidden with green shadows of plants. Luiza saw two golden lights. They were eyes. A black jaguar was watching her. She shivered with instinctive fear. The beautiful cat just observed her. No harm in the eyes. The cat-man smiled and softly said, "The prince of predators seems to like you. That is a good sign. You have some favor with cats."

"Yes, they come to me and have affection for me, and I for them." The shaman thought she might need this affection.

That night, as Luiza slept, the jaguar came and kept an eye on her. He came close to her, perceiving her features and her scent of woman. The golden-eyed visitor quietly departed well before sunrise.

During the second day, Luiza was becoming tired from the journey. Some sound was softly murmuring in her ears. "What is that? Do you hear it?"

"No, I do not. What is it?"

"It sounds like far off there is a voice. The voice of a little girl crying."

"Remember I told you about the dark one. He will enter your mind. He will want to talk to you in ways only you can understand. He knows things in your mind, and he can seduce you."

"It is a little girl crying. She is frightened and calling for her mother. She is lost and afraid in the jungle. I must help her."

"You were once lost and afraid in the jungle. He knows how to reach you down deep. The dark one will beguile you."

"I must help her." Tears entered her eyes. Anguish and confusion abounded.

"Rest here, Luiza. I will go to the stream for some water. Be still. Call upon your guardian spirits as I have taught you. Sing out to the spirit that loves you. Reject the dark one."

She watched the shaman disappear into the web of fauna like he had entered an ocean wave, blue and green. She was alone now. The moaning and crying became more distinct. She could almost see her beyond the wild plants before her. She saw her own soiled and terrified face as a little girl, crying, vulnerable, lost, and left behind.

A different voice came to her. It was the spirit voice of the eagle. "Be quiet now and calm yourself. I am here. Watch what I see from above." She could see the jungle below. It was immense and the light of the fading sun reflected off the canopy. The view now sharpened into a window into the green pool of foliage. She could see movement inside this opening.

She saw it clearly now. A child was seated on the ground. Her dark hair was tangled and twisted in knots. She was filthy, with smears of dried mud and debris over her slender naked body. Her hands were tied together tightly. Streaks from tears ran down her soiled face. There was a strap around her neck and secured to a tree branch above her. Not far away sat an old tattooed man with long black hair. His eyes shone like some creature that prowls the night. There were markings and small pierced objects on his face and torso. He was smiling with cruel satisfaction.

Luiza was moving swiftly now. The shadows began to creep over the green.

She stumbled and fell into a soft carpet of spongy moss and flowers.

There was the faint scent of cinnamon. A buzzing sound came from a nest of honeybees.

Luiza asked, "How can I save her?"

A clear voice spoke in her mind. "My friends, the bees, will not harm you. How can I help you?"

"There is a little girl over there. She is being held captive. Can you help me to save her?"

"This evil has been around here too long. The bees will find him."

Luiza stood up and raced into the jungle. There was a sound like the wind in a sandstorm. Above, she saw a flowing mass like smoke. She followed it.

Now she could hear a man's voice cursing, shouting, growling. There before her now was the tattooed old man. He was swinging wildly, jumping, then rolling on the ground. Bellowing with rage and pain, his body was covered by angry bees. His eyes and his mouth were attacked. He tried to scream. He fell to the ground and began shaking and convulsing. He tried to stand and yelled, "Make them stop!"

Luiza ran to the little girl. She was shivering with fright while staring in disbelief at the torrent of bees on her captor's body. Luiza said, "I have come to help you. You are safe now. I will take you home." The strap was untied, and Luiza carried her away. The evil man was moaning and had begun to die.

She ran away with the little girl in her arms until, exhausted, she had to stop. The child was quiet and in a state of shock. Her face was a mask of bewildered torment. Luiza could only guess what had happened to her. She spent a moment examining her body. She reeked of filth. Her skin was cut, scraped, and scabby. Her eyes were lost to some other world. The child screamed and fainted.

Somehow, Luiza carried her to the place the cat-man had been before he left to get water. The cat-man returned, appearing calm. He acknowledged the child and offered a bowl of water. Then he walked off to be alone. Luiza thought it strange he was so quiet and withdrawn.

She fed the child some water through her dry, chapped lips. The child swallowed and groaned. She moistened a bit of cloth and dabbed her sores and abrasions. There was blood around the girl's privates and around her thighs. The girl trembled, then fell into a state of collapse.

Luiza laid a blanket over the child and rested her own mind and body. The sounds of the evening jungle began to stir. Movement came from the tangled bushes and vines. She could not see anything there. Shadows grew, and the air became cooler. Luiza slept in exhaustion with the little girl beside her. No one noticed the shifting plants or the rustle of the leaves.

Luiza stirred in her sleep. The child was clutching her, though apparently still asleep. Something felt wrong. It was black as night. She could just see the reflection of a dark orange moon through the canopy. Then a shadowy form stood over her. Flashes like sparks flickered where the eyes must be. The shaman?

"I told you he would draw you to him. Why did you not wait for me? You are so stubborn and foolish. Look at me!" She rose up to see better. She saw his eyes glowing with a red flame.

"Is that you, shaman?"

"Not anymore. The bees killed my host, so now the old cat-man is my host. You didn't really believe the bees could kill me, did you? I am master here. That includes you and the little bitch with you. Now I will teach you about my ways. You are my slut and my puppet. The cat-man is mine, and he will use his only arm to bring you along."

He reached for Luiza and, with ferocious strength, pulled her up to his face. She could smell his fetid breath and looked into his flashing eyes. Luiza saw the face of a raging beast ready to pounce.

A roar came from behind the cat-man. They both looked to see the gold, predatory eyes of the jaguar. It lunged—white fangs gleaming, claws like daggers. The cat-man released Luiza, trying to fend off the attack. She heard a grunt and saw the jaguar's jaws close on his throat. He tried to force the mouth open with his only hand. Screaming and slobbering followed as the jaws tightened. The immense force of the bite only clenched deeper.

Luiza was just a body length away. She looked into the jaguar's eyes. The dark pupils widened, and she heard a voice in her head say, *"Take the girl and run—now!"*

CHAPTER 35 | SPAIN

It was dark and a clear night in northern Spain. The entire group had eaten and sat around a blue-yellow fire. George was at peace, looking into the blaze. Crackles and sparks from the roasting logs reminded him of those days of camping in the Ozarks with Rick.

"Remember I would play the guitar at our camp?"

George looked to his left, and Rick was there.

"Shit, you could give me a heart attack, Rick."

"Sorry, I just got here."

Suddenly then, the van rolled up some hundred meters away. The Zulus unloaded and bid farewell to Padre Raphael and the driver. As they made their way to the camp, George saw a light behind them. It was a woman walking behind them. The leader stopped and surveyed this sudden appearance. He listened to her and nodded his head. It was the woman from the jungle he saw in a dream. He understood she was present to assist them in their efforts to destroy the evil being. She had huge spirit power. He had been uncomfortable about this mission. He told his warriors about her in his dream. They all welcomed her with thanks and felt reassured. The men had shared their own fears about this beast.

***

Yellow-eyes lay in his new cave, licking his wounds. Awareness of familiar beings entered his mind. The woman in the jungle from long ago had arrived. The Zulus, who had experience in using spirits of nature to attack him, were perceived like smoke before the fire. That young man was here—the one he had done away with in the hospital. How he envied his courage and pure heart. He was jealous and resentful of all of them. The world had abandoned him. They had rejected him first. No one was there to protect him in his time of need. Like a green piece of fruit, he had been thrown on the ground to rot.

He would call upon his own gang of rejected spirits—dark spirits who understood the meaning of anger and defiance. All that talk about love and surrender to find peace of mind was a lie to control him and defeat him.

Asmodeus thought of the dark spirit known as Lucifer. *"That bastard even scares me,"* he muttered. *"I can try to summon him."* The fire's dark red coals gave off a dim glow. In the distance, a night owl called out—perhaps for a mate, or for prey. The air was crisp and clean. Overhead, stars shimmered, close enough to touch. Pale, creamy moonlight reflected off the nearly full moon.

Irony. The calm before the storm. The world, so brimming with life—only for death and tragedy to follow a day later. This drama had played out for millions of years. Billions, actually.

George's thoughts drifted to the senseless poverty, ignorance, and the filth of squalid ghettos. To the meaningless suffering of the sick. The forgotten children left behind during humanity's self-inflicted wars. Nature could be just as ruthless—violent, indifferent.But also breathtakingly beautiful. Always bursting with life, always struggling. For food. For water. For space and dominance. The Beast claims its prize; others fight to steal it.

As these thoughts swirled, George heard a melody rise in his mind: Ravel's *Pavane for a Dead Princess*.It was sweet and solemn. Tragic, yet full of quiet meaning—for those willing to listen. So much harmony. So much dignity. In that, George found a fragile hope. A reminder that life wasn't always bleak.

Sometimes he fell into that hollow place inside himself, convinced it was all just meaningless crap.And then he'd see a week-old fawn racing through a wildflower meadow—running for the joy of it.

He wondered: Why had so many people briefly died, only to return with stories of a life beyond their bodies? Most kept it to themselves, afraid of being mocked or told it was nothing more than brain chemistry. Over millennia, humans had accepted religion— with its gods, messiahs, angels, and souls. But George craved something more—evidence, reason.

Einstein had said, *"God does not play dice."*Yet quantum physics came along and whispered otherwise. Something *was* rolling dice—in the smallest corners of reality.

With a weary humility, George let out a deep sigh."Life is mysterious," he said softly.

Rick looked at him, his eyes catching the glow of the moon. "Yes, it is," he replied.

Sleep came quickly after that.

***

Asmodeus felt something among the rock-strewn floor of the cave. His claw-like fingers dug into the scree. It was smooth and had form. With a grunt he found purchase and pulled it out. It was barely visible in the moon glow. It was cool and flat and had six sides. It was a box or tiny chamber. Closer scrutiny revealed some color like tarnished metal. Rubbing it on his clothing, it shone more clearly. It was heavy for such a small box. The light sparkled off it. It was gold. It had a lid. He shook it. There was some movement inside. His soiled finger touched a peg protruding under the lip. It was a latch catch. With his fingernail he opened it with a click. He tried to smell it. No scent was present. There was a tiny red spark, then only a dark form inside. What is this? He held the form in his hand. It had weight. He jostled it in his grasp. With his thumb and two fingers he held it up to the cave entrance for light. It was elliptical and uniform.

Deep inside yellow-eyes, a primordial tingle became fear. A warning. Terror now grew inside him. "Now you've done it!" That voice. It was the darkest one on earth—Lucifer. "You are a filthy mess. Foul lusting with the humans again. You are on your own this time. You stink of filth. I will gather more souls willing to be my soldiers. Watch out for the animal spirits. They are coming for you."

Yellow-eyes trembled like a naked child in the jungle night. "But I thought you cared about me." Lucifer was gone.

***

George woke with a start. Where are you, Rick? He found him with Lobo. He was scratching his ear. Lobo was grinning and looking in Rick's eyes. "He appears to like you, Rick."

"I like this guy too. He is smart, gentle, and strong. We are going to find that asshole today."

"Who is that woman, Rick? Do you know her?"

"Her name is Luiza. I know her only a little. We were introduced. She is a teacher and here to help all of us. She is from the spirit home and knows a lot about animal and natural spirits. I saw her speaking to those African guys."

"I'm hungry. Let's eat a bite, Rick."

The entire group was together around the camp breakfast table. Manqoba asked, "What's the plan, Dr. Swisher?"

"I am a doctor and a researcher. I am not qualified to hunt down prey, least of all a cunning and evil being like this Asmodeus. I turn to experts for that. You and your men are the experts here."

Manqoba looked down at the ground and then above. He imagined his own home of South Africa with its natural beauty. "It is the same earth below and the same sun above. We have done this in other lands. We have found our quarry and delivered the evil ones before. My men and I have felt uncomfortable with this one. We will do it. But something is different here. The natural spirits are not so powerful here as those in Africa. The spirits here are more gentle. I am more confident since Luiza has arrived. Rick has a strength to him too. Luiza has told me it is not the strength we need. Please explain this, Luiza."

Luiza had a faint blue aura around her. She was calm and smiling. Her countenance shone with a humble cheer—the bright and affectionate teacher, knowing yet caring even more. "Come here, Lobo." His ears perked up. His tail was wagging. Strolling up to her, he sat and looked at her. Luiza stroked his head. "Tell me, Lobo, how will you find this foul creature they call yellow-eyes?" Lobo stood up, put his nose to the sky, and sniffed. He walked around the group. He then returned to Luiza's feet and sat. "Lobo will show us where he is hiding. He will not be asked to enter the lair. That will be the job of someone else. The experienced warriors will introduce themselves to yellow-eyes then." Pedro was glad to hear that.

***

George asked, "What have you learned over the time since you passed away in Evanston Hospital?" Rick looked up and away.

"To appreciate what I have. My spirit group is like my football team firing on all cylinders. I have learned about having faith in the Big Spirit who loves us. Remember we were told by Jesus, 'God loves the sparrow, and how much more does he love you?'"

"Yes, I remember. It is so easy to doubt it. After you died, Rick, my faith in God went down the drain. I became angry and wondered why a loving God allows this."

"I don't know, George. The elders know more about this. On earth, we have to live by the tooth and bone sometimes. After the storm, things quiet down again. Wisdom takes time and a lot of experience. My favorite spirit teacher likes to talk about love and then kicks my ass too. He says, 'You've got to do the job. If you get hurt and fail, try again and keep trying.'"

"Lobo is calling me, George. See you later." Rick was light on his feet and scampered off to find Lobo. George went over to the group for a cup of coffee. He saw the ladies gathered around Luiza.

"Good morning, Manqoba."

"I saw you speaking to this man called Ricky. He is your brother?"

"Yes, my older brother by three years."

"Where did he go?"

"Do you mean when he died?" Manqoba nodded his head yes.

"Rick has been in a spirit place, learning and sharing with his group. They come and go and share their experiences with each other. Elders are there to teach and lead too. Rick told me this yellow-eyes guy killed him when he was recovering in the hospital after surgery. Rick really wants to get his hands on him. He is strong and courageous, though I have never known him to be a vindictive person."

"Maybe I can meet him. He reminds me of my older brother Maurice. He was an athlete and musically talented too. He was murdered by somebody in a senseless act. He was stabbed in the back by a jealous drunk and just died."

"I am sorry for your loss, Manqoba. I will see if Rick can speak to you."

***

The sun was beginning to warm the morning. George noticed a change in the air. No birds, no breeze—too quiet. Manqoba was upset however, George didn't think much of it. Pre-hunt jitters. Then clear as a bell, Rick's words in his mind: "He has Luiza. Lobo is on the trail."

George ran over to the group and there was almost hysteria. "She never came back from the stream," said Diane. Manqoba was on full alert. This was not the same game now. This beast was clever and knew the territory. George yelled to Manqoba, "Rick says Luiza is with yellow-eyes. Lobo has the trail." The warrior men got their gear and were running up the hill. George was close behind them.

Luiza recalled going to the bushes near the stream. There was a flash of light and then darkness. She was now in a dark place. Being a spiritual being, this was very strange. She was being restrained. She felt his dark malice all over now. She was being raped spiritually. "I always get my way. Yes, you can be fucked spiritually." Something had paralyzed her. "It is even better this way. The pleasure I get and the defeat you find. Give me your soul." Luiza's pain was beyond physical. It was emotional and moral terror. Her spirit was draining away. Essential life, good love, healthy energy was leaving her soul. She looked into his eyes of predatory evil. They were burning with fire. Power and complete control.

Powerful beasts are often most vulnerable during sex. Something smashed into Asmodeus. It was Lobo—vicious slashing on his neck. Yellow-eyes grabbed Lobo's neck and felt the fangs dig deeper into him. He squeezed his fingers into the dog and with a mighty scream tore the jaws away from his throat. He threw Lobo against the stone wall with renewed brutal strength. Lobo's head struck the wall and he collapsed like a fur rug.

Another attack came. Spirit on demon. It was Rick. Unrestrained. Rick put all his strength into his fist that smashed yellow-eyes in the head. The Beast stumbled and fell to his knees. Rick pounced on him, his hands around the smelly neck. Luiza was free. She just stared, amazed.

George stood outside the cave opening. He had seen Rick enter the cave. A burst of light struck his eyes. What was that? He couldn't know that Rick had entered the dark spirit of Asmodeus with brutal power. Asmodeus glowed and then, with horrific terror, became a white-hot flame. All was quiet now. George looked over at Manqoba and his warriors. Raising his arm, Manqoba motioned for his men to enter the cave. It was dark there. A flashlight revealed shadows and steel gray walls. Further in revealed the body of Lobo crumpled on the floor. George followed behind and saw three human bodies lying on the stones. One was still moving. It was Luiza.

"Help me, George," was in his mind. Rick's voice. George rushed forward.

"I hear you, Rick." Manqoba went to Luiza, picked her up, and carried her back to his men. Manqoba said, "Do not touch them, George. They are still in struggle. We cannot see it. It is in the spirit place." Understanding this, he said, "I'm here, Rick. I'll do anything for you. Just let me know."

George heard Rick say, "Something has me and won't let me go. A rope or a line of sticky light is around me."

"Manqoba, something is holding Rick back from getting away." Manqoba barked out to his warriors to come forward. "Surround the bodies. Bring the lion claw." A saber-like claw was revealed from a leather pouch. "Place it on Rick's chest, Kaboa." The men began to chant and sing. They were calling for the lion beast spirit. A red glow appeared around the claw. It became ruby red, and the glow entered Rick's body.

George heard screams in his mind. There was a tremendous roar and then a scream of terror. The lion spirit had captured the stump-man spirit. Horrible roars and ragged breathing led to another wailing scream. Kaboa said, "He has the dark evil spirit now. It is a fight to the death." The roars grew more intense, then a pleading howl sounded in George's mind. Then all was quiet. The red glow returned to the claw on Rick's chest. Kaboa picked it up and returned it to the pouch. Rick's body became a glow of blue. He was alive and opened his eyes. George knelt beside his brother. "I am here, Rick."

Manqoba was holding Lobo. "This dog has great courage." Luiza went to the lifeless dog. She placed her hands around his head. She cried for his spirit and thanked him for helping to save her. Another warrior took the dog in his arms and carried him out of the cave. Manqoba steadied Luiza, and they followed behind.

George held onto Rick's body in the dark cave. "What happened, Rick?"

"My spirit collided with the demon spirit. He let go of Luiza. But then I was being drawn into him. This is still new to me. My use of brute force may not be the best. No prior experience for me on a spiritual level for this. I am tired. Like after a convulsion."

"Where did you go?" asked George.

"A dark place and emotionally cold. There was a roar of some beast. Then howling and screaming. I was released then. Here I am."

"You are safe now, here with me, Rick."

"George, I must leave now. My spirit guide is calling for me to come to our place of rest. One thing to say. I have met with Mother, and she is spiritually more healthy now. She loved us, and I realize her soul was not healthy enough to always be a stronger mother for us. She loves you. Someday you will know this too. Now I will leave. I love you and will see you again. Of this, I am sure."

And he was gone. His body left with him. The demon body was nowhere to be found. George arose and made his way out to the sunshine over St. James Way.

CHAPTER 36 | UNITED STATES

George was back in the States again. A deep emptiness filled him. Filled up with the blues. Did the soldier surviving a war feel like this? He went to a meeting. A spoonful of spiritual nourishment. The grip of self-pity, anger, and hopelessness had a hold on him. Get out and do something.

A program was interrupted on the news that Israel had a nuclear bomb dropped on Tel Aviv. Millions were dead. Life on Earth was no longer the same.

Who did it? What will happen now? George stared in disbelief. All bets were off now. There was only conjecture as to who did this. Would the Muslim mortal enemies of Israel really do this? This was not just a terror attack. It came with higher authority. Nuclear warheads that wiped out a city were delivered with the go-sign of a major power. The attack came around 3 a.m. Tel Aviv time, and the blast occurred above the city to maximize destruction. The radioactive fallout would kill thousands or millions more. The nuclear fingerprint would point to the arsenal from which it was born.

A phone call came in, startling George. "Hello?" It was Manqoba.

"Do you know who did this?"

"How the heck would I know?" said George.

"The repercussions on Earth will be immense," said Manqoba.

"Why are you calling me?"

"The Zulu elders have agreed this has the appearance of more than just a human act. It is my belief as well that the Dark One has a role in this. A warrior told me that a spirit spoke to him in a dream. It warned that the Dark One was in the very cave in Spain the day before we were there."

"What was in the dream message?"

"Lucifer had scorned Asmodeus and refused to help him. It seems Lucifer had more important business to attend to."

"Are you suggesting Lucifer was the author of this horrible mess?" Manqoba said yes.

"Why are you sharing this with me?"

"I need your help, George. We need to find a way to be sure what we suspect is happening and then share it with the powers that be. For some reason, the dream requested your assistance in these days that come."

"Shit, there goes my plans for a final knock-down, fall-down, get-drunk-as-a-skunk."

"Not now, George," said Manqoba.

***

"So forgiveness is the answer? Tell me, Sara." Netanyahu was crippled with rage. They were in Brussels, where a conference was to be held entitled "Peace in the Holy Land." It was cancelled. His wife was exhausted, in tears.

"Why would our maternal queen have come to me? It happened!" she wailed.

Premier Netanyahu said, "An eye for an eye. Remember the Torah. That is our lesson. The Mossad will soon know who destroyed our Tel Aviv and over one million inhabitants. Rachmana Litzlan!" (God help us!)

***

"You tell me what the fuck happened! God damn it! Find out who pulled the trigger. All resources. No holds barred. NSA, CIA, FBI, IAEA. Oh God. We must know." The U.S. President was in a rage. "How could they get a nuclear bomb over Israel without anyone even lifting a finger?"

"We just don't know yet. We're working on it," said the Secretary of Defense. "The Muslim nations are the likely first suspects. But even some terrorists could have somehow done this."

"No more speculation. All that data. Billions in equipment. God help us all and our children."

His personal secretary entered and said, "Mr. President, PM Netanyahu is calling again. Will you take it?"

"Yes, I will."

President Putin said, "God keeps those safe who keep themselves safe." The GRU and military high command were in a lavish conference room in the Kremlin. President Putin stared at the GRU commander. He recalled the early death of General Sergun at age 58. A lot of bungled events like the downing of flight MH17 over Ukraine. Now the role was held by the newly appointed General Alexei Dyumin. He was an old friend from Putin's days as a hockey player and fellow member of the KGB, now called SBP.

President Putin needed information, and he needed it fast. Could this bomb possibly be one from Russia's own arsenal?

"Alexei, the trail of nuclear fallout could tell the world a story that could come to haunt us. All of your skills are to be used to find out where this weapon came from and who used it."

"Yes, Mr. President." In General Dyumin's experience of investigation, sometimes there really was a monster behind that locked door.

In the darkened shadows of his private study, the Ayatollah was on his knees. He prayed for guidance and tearfully began to believe he must be insane.

"Allah, with sadness I have failed to follow your wishes. My soul may now be lost to the unclean and foul darkness of Satan's chambers. You know more than me that the General disobeyed my orders and delivered the bombs."

***

In the once vibrant center of Tel Aviv, the thirty-four-story apartment building had crumbled into a smoldering heap. Rebecca once played with her four-year-old brother Joshua on the 28th floor apartment. Her six-year-old body had been vaporized by the stellar hot furnace of the hydrogen bomb. Where were they?

The spirit of Rebecca was quite well and alive. She had recalled the blinding flash and then a sensation of flying into a gentle flow of violet warmth. The place was surrounded by love and safety. Her favorite grandmother was with her now. She was aglow with soothing protective affection. Somewhere in this place were the spirits of Joshua, her mother, and father.

***

Who are you, Lucifer? Where is your soul? What are you? A mother grieves for her newborn baby. Born empty of life. The gazelle, barely standing now, born one hour before. The leopard hunting snatches it and carries it up into a tree. A lonely gorilla finds a kitten and loves it.

CHAPTER 37

The Iranian general had committed suicide. The pilots who delivered the bombs returned safely to the secret mountain air base. The Dark One surveyed the scene. It was now just a blemish on the Israeli coast. Tick tock. Now would come the tradition of an eye for an eye. His heritage was not unlike many before or after. The spiritual energy that formed his soul came from the same great pool of creation that formed all souls. Someone had to do this job. To lead can be a lonely life. The others described him as defiant and full of rage. The elders of the spirit world had never encountered such a powerful and furious young spirit before.

He had left the spiritual nest eons ago. He missed the love of kind maternal and paternal souls. He found self-love was more reliable. The pleasure of dominion over other human spirits was the most satisfying reward of all.

Just as he had convinced the Persian general to execute the plan, he would go to the Zionist warrior in command. The PM and his wife were not obedient to him. Strike while the iron is hot.

Satan entered ground zero in spirit form. There was pleasure in knowing his plan was working. Fires still burned, and the buildings were just charred blocks of concrete and shards of twisted steel. Further along, he could see blackened corpses. Nothing was alive. The wind blew unobstructed. The smell of death was all around. "Now it is time for the Jews to return the favor."

It was best to go to the military, who already had the necessary tools and keys. One stealth bomber with two 12-megaton bombs was ready. The perfect pilot had been chosen. He was a colonel in the Israeli Air Force—very obedient, trustworthy, and trained to deliver strategic weapons anywhere in the region.

Satan called the colonel on his satellite phone. Using the voice of the pilot's commanding officer, he gave him the necessary security codes. He told him to take off with armed weapons immediately. "Fly below radar until out of Israeli airspace, climb to 60 thousand feet in full stealth vestige. Then go directly to the target area of Tehran. Drop the bombs there." The pilot was convinced it was the voice of his commanding officer. Ground personnel were ordered to make all preparations for the immediate flight.

Satan returned the satellite phone to his pocket. He calmly continued his stroll through the ruins of Tel Aviv. He dressed in an Israeli officer's uniform. He entered the remains of a hospital. Mangled, blackened bodies offered no greeting. Their spirits were on their return journey to their other homes or already there.

A confirming bleep was heard on the satellite phone in his pocket. The colonel was acknowledging the message and now following orders.

George considered going to the liquor store. It was just a short drive to that carwash with a liquor supply. Open on Sundays too. The good old days. "Like hell!" He used to get the 'I-don't-care' attitude, buy a bottle, and go to his hideout. His pet cats seemed to approve. No more pets, no more booze now.

Instead, he took a walk. At the entrance to the grocery store, he saw that fat gypsy lady. She owned that spot. "Are you a gypsy, ma'am?"

"For the poor, please. I have children hungry and sick. God will love you for helping. I am not a gypsy, no. I am a poor mother wishing to feed my children." George could see coins and green bills in the glass jar.

"I wonder who will help all the people dying or about to die from the bombs? God help us learn how to live in peace," said George. He put a dollar in the jar. The gypsy lady thanked him.

"God of my understanding, please guide me in Your will for me. I do not know what I can possibly do for this catastrophe."

"George, the elders have asked you to help out." It was Rick in his mind. "My mentor chewed me out for jumping in on that asshole in the cave. The elders intervened. They said the rules have changed. If humans are to move forward on Earth, they need help now. The weapons of mass destruction in the hands of people operating on medieval traditions just don't get it." George thought about Carl

Sagan's warnings of intelligent life forms destroying each other if they could not get past this critical step. "What is it, Rick?"

"Remember Dad used to say the hardest part is just showing up sometimes?"

"Yeah, I remember that."

"They suggest you travel to South Africa. The Zulus will be awaiting you. Luiza and I will be there too."

"OK, Rick."

***

The Chinese supreme leader Xi Jinping was not known to be emotionally dramatic. He had a warm smile and the countenance of a good-natured father. He had made friends during his travels with most of the Asian and European countries he visited. Japanese-Chinese relations were an exception. President Xi made a call to President Putin to discuss the Tel Aviv massacre. He needed some measure of how his neighbor was reacting to this crisis. Both spoke through translators.

"Our estimates are that two 10-megaton nuclear bombs were detonated," said Xi. "The devastation of the Tel Aviv metropolitan area was up to a ten-mile radius in all directions from downtown central. Loss of primary strike life is estimated to be over one million lives."

President Putin understood this was a search for a reaction. "President Xi, the search for who delivered this awful attack has begun. The survival of my own country and even the whole of civilized mankind is in question. I will be meeting with the ambassadors of the major powers here in Moscow. I will be speaking with the Ayatollah on a secure phone today. The Israeli ambassador has been overwhelmed. He apparently lost some family in the blast."

Xi said, "I wonder what can be done to the perpetrators. The Israelis are likely to want revenge and more. It is my hope that some dialogue is underway even as we speak, between Israel and the Americans. There are over one billion people in my country who deserve an explanation and some assurance of safety."

Putin responded, "My friend, your words are mine. I truly fear for my country as well as the entire population on this planet."

"Thank you, President Putin. I share your concerns. Let us talk more later."

***

The flight to South Africa was less than one hour from landing in Durban. Listening to his favorite classical guitar pieces by Albéniz, George reflected on beauty. Green blush over the spring sunlit fields of Andalusia. Perfect melody and harmony of Clair de Lune by Debussy. A month-old colt racing in the pasture on her magical long legs. The second kiss of his first love when he was six years old. Watching Bo Jackson run for a 60-yard touchdown to win the game. Faith in a Supreme Being that he did not understand.

The modern scholars of science and philosophy said there really is no evil. It is the absence of good health or nurturing that we see in murderers. It is fear that releases violent, malicious behavior. There is no essential evil. It is ignorance and misunderstanding that incite vindictive destruction.

CHAPTER 39

Manqoba met George at the airport. The journey to the small countryside village lasted an hour by car. The background of mountains and forest brought calm and peace to him. They ate a light meal and sat out on the terrace. It was just the two of them.

"My brother Maurice and I could sit out here for hours, talking and listening to music. How are you now, George?"

"Much better now. The breeze is fresh and I hear the sounds of the country. The home is beautiful. I don't sleep well when I travel over time zones in an easterly direction. I may have a better chance of sleeping here."

"We will speak with a group of elders tomorrow. Luiza spoke to someone doing his chores at his ranch. It is not clear what we must do. Let us sleep now."

***

He entered a deep, restful sleep. He was exhausted from the flight.

Rick began, "It is too late to intervene in the destruction that will occur. The Dark One has more influence than we have time to prepare. I will visit the Zulu group with you and Luiza. We need patience and preparation to get this Satan shithead. I am your brother in spirit as well as blood. Remember that."

George continued to sleep. The message was softly received.

Sara was in a state of torment and despair. She collapsed onto the bed. She was still in Brussels. The room had a glow of soft sapphire blue. The matriarch, Sarah, had come again.

"Hard lessons for the people of Earth."

"Grandmother, my heart cannot bear this burden. I have lost loved ones and Bibi has gone to seek the only justice he knows. His wrath is beyond any I have ever seen before."

"Your spirit cousins are trying to bring this violence and hatred to a close. Hard lessons. The Dark One has his own agenda. The elder spirits have been struggling against this evil for eons. The Beast and his dark army persist like a plague. How can there be cleanliness without filth? Remember, Sister Sara, more battles will be fought. Some won, some lost. Never give up!"

It became known that the nuclear bombs were from the old Soviet Union reactor in Mayak near the Arctic Circle. How it was obtained and delivered was not known or shared. The Mossad learned that satellite data from the NSA indicated the aircraft to drop the bombs was likely from a remote airfield in the northwestern mountains of Iran. The suicide of the Iranian general the day after the attack contributed to the theory Iran did it. Netanyahu had been taken to a secure underground facility to meet with his military and intelligence council. Jerusalem was evacuated of all non-security personnel. There was great paranoia over the likelihood of a second attack. Mossad agents in Iran and throughout the world were searching for answers. Preparations were being made to carry out a strategic counterattack when the order came.

CHAPTER 40

Msizi was the high priest of the Zulu village. His experience could best be described as that of a seer. It was he who was spoken to by Luiza during his chores on his ranch. He had been told to gather the Zulu warriors. Msizi had many years of experience reading messages from the animal and plant spirits. Being a farmer in life, he felt at home with nature. He often went alone into the forest to commune with the ancient world of plants and animals. The autumn of the southern hemisphere abounded in great varieties of natural life.

The message given to him telepathically included a view of a smoky valley of debris from crushed and smoldering buildings. He was frightened by this. He believed he was seeing the next city to be decimated. It was not Tel Aviv.

***

As a guest, George was seated in a sturdy wooden chair near the front row. Maurice was beside him. The modest hut was built of wooden floors and walls. The roof was thick, piled thatch. Soft morning light entered the small windows. Sculpted masks with native faces hung on the walls. A painting hung on a wall revealing a lion surrounded by colorful fauna and a soaring eagle above.

About twelve members of this village were in attendance. In front and facing them was Msizi, with the same warriors seen in Spain. George sensed somebody sitting behind him. It was Luiza. To her right sat Rick. He saw the gleam in Rick's eye and a smile. George felt better immediately. He reached over and held his hand for a moment.

Msizi spoke. "I saw it in the vision. A valley with mountains nearby. The valley was blackened and leveled into chunks of stone and steel. No trees or green. It was a dead city. The city is Tehran. It will happen just as the vision predicts. Visions such as these are from the spirit world that gives a view of the future. I am sharing this with you in hopes that we can respond together. There is a waterfall ten miles into the forest. We can go there to combine our strengths with nature. Human life came out of this African wilderness. Let us call upon this nature for the renewed power we need."

***

Three vans in various states of disrepair bumped and stumbled along the narrow pass into the dense forest. Rick was looking like the young man last seen in Spain: strong, determined, with a sparkle in his eye.

"George, your presence is needed. To the world you are a nobody except with enough earthly experience to make some sense of what is happening. The world powers that be need someone to explain it to them. The Dark One is a nightmare for all concerned. My spirit guide and the elders have seen the need to step up. We need to convince this Lucifer shithead to disappear."

"I will show up and do what I can, Rick." George looked out on the forest and valley as they rocked along. Not a lot of progress had been made in forensic psychiatry. Labels on mental illness were a fancy way of classifying this or that. Some large-scale social deviance had occurred in the last century. The origin of this destructive behavior on a grand human scale was unclear. They were called sociopaths. The Dark One may be called a spiritual sociopath. How did that happen? The time had come to fight back at whatever one called it.

Luiza looked at George. She said, "Some of this will work itself out. We have to do our jobs. The spirit world is convinced there is enough good in human beings to be more active in their struggles to survive. Rick and I have a plan to offer. The Zulus have a unique blend of experience and skill to make this work."

***

The idea of psychopathic spirits brought chills to George. Bad enough there were humans like this. The real boogeyman in the background was this unseen evil. Can't fight it if you can't find it.

The vans had arrived at the waterfall. The air was fresh and humid. Light sparkled off a mist. The drop was about one hundred feet. The flow burst from a cave in the cliff. The waterfall was crystal clear. A blue glow gently surrounded its passage to enormous smooth boulders below. The collection of water formed a wide, transparent pond. Birds of green and red darted around the pond.

The group settled in a clearing downstream from the fall. Msizi began with a prayer to the spirits of the forest.

"Fresh water, sunlight, and earth combined to bring life for all. The visions I have received have disturbed this peace. Zulu people are people of the light and sky. We worship the creator of this place and all that inhabit it. I speak to the good spirits now about the darkness. We are here for guidance. Some evil entity surely has a role in the death and destruction I have seen. Guide us in what we can do to turn back this evil presence."

A flock of the brightly colored birds had gathered on a rock ledge above the pool below. They were still and observant. More native birds, larger and darker in color, were silently landing on ledges further above. Down below, a dark hole in the wall suggested there may be a cave. Two golden marble eyes peered out. They blinked and quickly reappeared.

Luiza spoke to Rick. "Do you see the eyes below?"

He looked and said, "Yes, I see them."

She said, "It is the leopard of this valley."

There were swirls of movement in the water below. Beneath the soft turbulence, a school of fish was forming. Flashes of silver and red appeared. Towering over the group, a majestic tree stood strong and silent. George gazed above and saw movement. A mass of dark blue carpeted the armpit of a limb. Wasps were busy around their nest.

At that very moment, a nuclear blast occurred over Tehran. Just as Msizi had seen in his nightmare vision, the devastation spread out like a tsunami. The blinding flash lit the entire city and valley brighter than the sun. Over one million inhabitants never awakened again that day. The youngest son of the general who had committed suicide days before melted in his crib. Only the plume of smoldering mushroom-shaped plasma and gas could be seen from fifty miles away by a human being. A shepherd named Amir looked up from his disturbed flock of sheep. He spoke in his native Farsi, "Khoda nakone." (God forbid.)

Msizi had seen something else in his vision. He observed a beast approaching them from the waterfall. It was a black leopard. It stood over the cliff looking down on the pool. With precision and graceful balance, it leaped from rock to crevice to ledge and softly landed on the edge of the pond. Its coat was gleaming, black, and perfectly groomed. The eyes were brilliant, piercing yellow. It lapped cold water from the pool.

Msizi knew this was not an ordinary leopard. It was the Beast in a beautiful disguise. It had come to strut before the group. The dark Beast was very proud to have started a nuclear holocaust. The plan was simple enough: Destroy all human hope. Disrupt any chance for goodness and happiness to succeed. If the Dark One was to be excluded and denied his need for domination, then he would take it.

"We have an uninvited guest. I saw it in my vision. His presence is why we are here. If my vision was correct, it foretold the destruction of Tehran. He has come here to tell us about it. It may be that Tehran has already been bombed. As we have seen before, dark spirits have a need for recognition."

CHAPTER 41

Sleek and proud, the black leopard gracefully approached the edge of the pond opposite the group. The Dark One sat and almost smiled. He looked at the warriors, Luiza, Rick, and George. Msizi called out, "Are you satisfied now?" In their minds, they heard, "It is only the beginning. I will now let humans do the rest. See if the loving creator cares enough to save you!" Luiza and Rick observed movement in the tree above. Msizi had called upon a friend. The wasps were buzzing like an electric power line. A dark cloud of wasps was forming within the dense foliage of their tree. It was a boiling, festering swarm. The Dark One looked up. His ears tweaked to the strange buzzing sound. The Zulu warriors knew it was time to move.

Msizi gave the word to Manqoba, and the warriors ran downstream. The proud leopard was alert and enjoying the start of events. He did not notice the female leopard coming out of her lair. She leaped forward and sank fangs and claws around the neck of the Dark One. A shriek of fear and rage resounded off the canyon walls. The game had begun.

The black leopard leaped straight up, twisting like an angry snake going into a corkscrew. A vicious scream made George cringe. The larger black cat tore the female off his back and charged her. She cowered back into a gap in the rocks. He reached in with outstretched claws to drag her out. The cloud of wasps dove like a Stuka upon him. His mouth, nose, eyes, and ears were seething with a stinging mass. Another muffled howl was heard. The venom was inside the leopard, burning like fire. Another scream of pain, and he leaped for the water.

He dove for the safety of deeper water. Now the rolling flurry of fish was all around him. They attacked his skin with sharp predatory needle teeth. The warriors had reached the water's edge near the Beast. They waited for the Dark One to try to escape the churning fish attack. They had razor-sharp spears with them. Fish were snapping and chewing all around the Dark One's body. Barely able to find purchase on the rocky bottom, the cat climbed onto the shore.

The warriors were ready and waiting. Their spears entered his body without mercy. Fear and defeat were seen in his once-proud eyes. The Dark One knew it was time to leave. He was finding out what it meant to knock on death's door. He had one more trick. He would give up the ghost and slink away in spirit. As the spirit seeped out, a screeching flutter of birds was waiting. They entered his confused soul space. The birds somehow knew where to fly and disturb the faltering spirit. The sadistic soul of this evil spirit could find no relief. Birds continued to disrupt his efforts to leave.

At this moment, Luiza and Rick made their attack. Now in their blue aura, they departed from their bodies. Like two laser beams of light, they struck the evil spirit simultaneously. A brilliant flash of red and orange appeared with a deafening boom. The air just snapped and sizzled, and then became quiet. The birds flew to their roost. The wasps returned to their nest. The water became still and smooth. The female leopard silently crept away into the forest.

Msizi called the warriors back. He said, "Thank you, Mother Nature, for your help." George could find no trace of Luiza or Rick. They gathered up and returned to the village.

CHAPTER 42

George had fallen off to sleep after returning to the village. Outside his bedroom window, the night noises of insects and leaves rustling from the wind gave comfort to his weary sleep. Exhaustion from days and weeks of mental and emotional turmoil had taken their toll. Empty peace of a sleep well-earned.

None of them, the Zulus or George, knew what happened to the Dark One. Rick and Luiza had been chosen by the elders to do a job. And Mother Nature pitched in. What they were learning is that some spirits are 'gone bad.' The recent bad spirit wasn't the ultimate Angel of Darkness. He was one of the worst of many over the ages. As in mortal life, there are people 'gone bad' or bad to the bone. They need to be recognized and removed. Sometimes, if the corruption isn't too deep, a spirit can still be redeemed. The work of Manqoba, the forest spirits, the Zulu warriors, George, and finally Rick and Luiza was doing damage control. The spirit of the Dark One was on a one-way trip to the beginning—the resource for spiritual beings to be. Raw material. But that soul would never exist again.

During the depth of his sleep, George was provided some briefing. Luiza and Rick spoke softly to him. "Now it is your job to speak with the people who can influence others about the truth of what is happening. What is needed is a new understanding among human beings if they are to survive as a species." Without waking, George received further instructions about who to see and where to go. It was just the beginning of a new turn in humanity's struggle to survive.

He awoke as though returning from the sleep of the dead. Sunlight beamed around the edges of the curtain into the dust-speckled room. Breathe deep. Anxiety began to creep into his mind. Something to do. Oh yeah. Instructions from Luiza and Rick. George began to feel dread. "I am a nobody. Who will listen to me? I will be rejected or sent off to a hospital for the insane." Then he remembered it is not his job to convince anybody. Just deliver the message. Get help from others. They did say others will help. Just show up, George.

He cleaned up and got some breakfast. Coffee and juice. Toast and jelly. He spoke to Manqoba and thanked him. He gave Msizi a hug with heartfelt respect and gratitude. Msizi knew that George was troubled. "The spirits always help us if we ask. The maternal love of nature is available. One must ask for it and be strong. Our ancestral spirits, like Rick, will help us." George thanked each warrior and made his way to pack and leave. Even after seeing his brother again and seeing him help others, George still doubted that he would receive help if he just asked.

Millions were dead in Israel and Iran. Millions more would die from the radiation effects. And a world war may have already begun. George recalled the whispered words of Rick last night. "Go to China and speak to their supreme leader." George mumbled something about knowing enough Chinese to order Moo Goo Gai Pan.

CHAPTER 43

President Xi had not slept well for days. He was not his usual strong and steady self. The military was on high alert. Paranoia was in the air. The borders were tightened. Satellite reconnaissance data could only confirm the smoking debris in the Mideast. He had spoken with the ambassadors of Iran and Israel. They were no help. No one seemed to know who gave the orders. No one was taking responsibility. What a mess. Netanyahu denied ordering the strike on Tehran. The Ayatollah denied approving the release of bombs over Tel Aviv.

President Xi had been a stalwart Communist Party Chinese patriot. The survival of China was his priority. He was level-headed, rational, and a survivor of the political cleansing of reformed China. He was not inclined to superstition and not likely to believe that China had a world empire destiny. Somewhere in China's remarkable five thousand years of history, the idea of Great Destiny had been born and nurtured in the political soul of China. His faith was in hard work, economies of scale, and carrying a very big stick.

Sitting at his desk in his office, President Xi reviewed the day's schedule. He was to speak by phone with the Russian president, the U.S. president, the Iranian president, and then the ambassador of India in person. He heard soft speech in his native dialect. He looked up and around his office. Nobody was there. He looked at the computer screen, the phone, and then the overhead speaker.

"Please relax and just listen. Humor me, if you will. You are the only one who can hear me. I want you to tell your personal secretary to hold all calls while you go to your personal study for a while. Will you do it?" President Xi was not one who had ever heard voices before. He began to twitch and sniffed his cup of tea. Was someone playing a trick or practical joke on him?

"If you will only play along for a few minutes, I will explain everything."

Xi said, "Who are you? Is this some kind of spy device?" The voice just chuckled a bit.

"Please be quiet and just do as I say. My identity will be clear to you when you see me in your study. OK? You are safe, and believe it or not, I am your friend."

That did it. Now he was more than curious. He told his secretary to hold the calls while he was in his study. But first, he picked up his letter opener and put it in his pocket. On his way, he looked in the mirror to see if he was really doing this. He saw the weird expression on his face, and it startled him. He touched his face to be sure he was real. His pupils were wide, and his skin looked pale. Sheepishly, he tiptoed towards his study. He looked behind him and then at the closed door to his study. He tapped on the door.

The soft voice said, "Come in."

In Mandarin, Xi whispered, "Oh shit."

He cracked open the door and peeked inside. Sitting there was an old Chinese gentleman dressed in traditional robes. The old man had a Fu Manchu mustache and a long beard.

"Please come in, Mr. President." He looked around the room and saw no one else.

"Relax, Xi. Come sit with me. I am here to help you."

Xi said, "How did you get in here?"

"Have a seat. I made some tea for us. Do you like sugar in it?"

"No, thank you. Just plain. Who are you? What do you want?"

"I am Confucius. Please excuse my informal introduction. More specifically, I am the soul of the philosopher that lived in China two thousand years ago. This body looks similar to who I was physically. I am still that same spirit, though I hope more spiritually evolved now. Did you study any of my teachings?"

"I have always admired your teachings. But how do I know you are who you say you are?"

"Please remove the letter opener from your coat pocket. Yes, I know it is there."

Xi blushed. "I meant no harm, sir. I am nervous."

"Not to worry. I am the uninvited guest. I am sorry. Let me try to explain this situation." Xi seemed to relax and sat down. He placed the letter opener on the table. He appeared humbled though skeptical. The claim he was the spirit of Confucius was not convincing to Xi.

Confucius spoke, "Your doubt is still evident and reasonable. I have asked another soul to join us."

Another man appeared behind Xi near the door. He was dressed in a modern business suit. He entered and sat down. There was something very disturbing to Xi. He stared in disbelief. The man was a perfect copy of his father.

"Yes, my son, I am still alive and living in the afterlife. Do you recall how I used to secretly encourage you to keep an open mind? Remember how we used to wrestle and practice our balance and footwork?"

Xi's mouth was stuck open. His eyes were staring in disbelief. Tears began to form. His face was trembling.

"I am very proud of you, son. Do not try to touch me now. Please listen to our great-grandfather Confucius. I love you and your daughter too."

Crying now, "I will, Father."

The great Chinese teacher began to explain their coming here.

"Humans on Earth are now able to use the energy of atoms to either move forward or destroy civilization. We are spiritual beings that have earthly lives to learn and to grow. Destruction of the Earth and humanity eliminates our purpose for living—to grow closer toward our Creator. There is still hope that good leaders like you can help your people to move beyond selfish fear and aggression.

This is a pivotal time in man's evolution. A man will ask to visit you in the very near future. He has observed important events leading up to and surrounding the Mideast tragedy. His name is George. Consider him an envoy offering insights to you and others.

He is just a man and originally from America. What he has seen is important. He is not a spy or a harm. He is just a messenger. Listen to him and gather your staff together. See what you can do to help stop this cycle of violence. We are always nearby to support you. Goodbye for now."

And then they were gone.

President Xi looked around in stunned silence. "Who will believe me? They may want to put me away." He had enough presence of mind to return to his office. He told his secretary to schedule a meeting with his top available advisors in 24 hours. He personally called a security officer to facilitate the arrival and welcome of this person. "Please tell me when he will arrive."

***

Exhausted after a long day of flying, George gazed out the window at the vast modern city, home to more than twenty million people. To his relief, two sharply dressed men in uniform greeted him upon arrival. One of them, speaking English, welcomed him to China and informed him that President Xi had been expecting him.

George was escorted to a five-star hotel in a limousine, bypassing customs entirely. For the first time in hours, he began to feel a sense of relief—almost happiness. He even felt a bit special. He was told that President Xi and his staff would be meeting with him the following day.

George fell into bed and slept deeply. Rick came to him in a dream. They were fishing again along a mountain stream. Rick said, "Remember, showing up can be the hardest part. I will be nearby if you need me at the meeting."

"Thanks, Rick."

***

Feeling recharged and only a little disoriented the next day, George was taken by limousine to the meeting location. He was told it was a place called Zhongnanhai, with beautiful gardens and lakes. A modern office building stood out over the gardens. He was led into the building by his security escort. George felt like the royal guest. He arrived at the meeting feeling a bit diminutive. He did not speak Chinese. The president actually met him at the door. He spoke some English.

He was led to his seat beside President Xi. George was offered coffee or tea. He chose coffee. About twenty other people were present. Some were women.

The president began the meeting speaking in his native Mandarin dialect. George wore a tiny earpiece and heard perfect

English. He was astonished to hear that President Xi had received two spiritual visitors the day before. Looking around the table, he saw the faces of people staring in disbelief. Some smiled while others seemed stunned with concern. Did he just say that Confucius and his own father had met with him? Xi now turned to George and introduced him. He was sincerely interested in hearing what this guest had to say.

For just a moment, George had to comment on what the President had said. "Ladies and gentlemen, I believe exactly what President Xi said really happened. Whether it is his courage or out of necessity, I gratefully respect his candor. Over the last several days, I have witnessed and experienced some events I now share. These events pertain directly to the Mideast tragedy. It is my hope that we can interrupt and prevent further disasters which might lead to our annihilation." George took a deep breath and began his description of what happened in South Africa and Spain. He told it in a simple, matter-of-fact way. He did not try to convince anyone. He did not apologize for it. He did say his own brother helped to rid us of some evil beings and that Rick had died nearly 50 years ago.

***

"Humans are at a critical point in time. Our spiritual families and friends have stepped up to help us. It has happened before in history when prophets and wise ones appeared to help move things along." George paused. A very stern-faced general spoke. "Excuse my interruption. I have known President Xi a long time and trust him. However, I have learned over many years of intrigue and violent espionage to never trust anyone totally. Especially this stranger here and some old man that claimed to be Confucius. This could all be some elaborate scheme to divert our attention from an imminent attack. Maybe the CIA or the Russians are behind this."

The door behind George opened, and the old man Confucius entered. "Fair enough, General Chang. It is wise to be cautious." General Chang had a nervous habit of tapping his finger on the table when he was upset. His right index finger was tapping like a piston just then. A voice entered Chang's mind.

"Boy, stop picking your nose." It was his mother's voice. He looked around the room as though to say, "Did you hear that?" But he didn't say that. His face turned as red as his uniform. He felt like a naughty child. Confucius said, "You heard someone speaking to you just now, didn't you?" The General looked at him with sheep's eyes. "Shall I tell them who it was and what was said?" The General almost pleaded when he said, "No."

***

Confucius continued, "I am the spirit once having lived in China about two thousand years ago. I have returned here to explain that our mortal lives are very important. Our souls live on after our physical death. We will return to Earth for another life when the time is right. Our purpose is to grow towards the likeness of our Creator. Simply put, human life can choose to destroy itself or choose to grow into more mature, evolved beings. We are all kindred spirits, and humans need help. Listen to George. Think about it. Make wise choices." Confucius disappeared.

George tried to continue. The audience was agitated. There was loud talk and shouting. President Xi intervened. He asked them to take a break, to reflect among themselves. General Chang rose from his chair and left the room. All of them stood up and began moving about. The room began to buzz with chatter.

***

President Xi brought the meeting to order after the break. "Everyone must have strong feelings, doubts, fears, real questions, and disturbing reactions to what we have heard. George has not come here to tell us what to do. He has delivered his message and experiences. Would someone like to ask a question?" A small woman with large glasses stood up. "I am Dr. Lui, a physicist and a military consultant. Yes, we can deliver devastation throughout the civilized world. Only the evil or insane want that. If we are spiritual beings and living in a physical world, what does it matter how we destroy this world if our spirits will live on?"

George struggled with this very same question. A little voice in his head said, "You showed up, now give it your best shot." He began, "Dr. Lui, you know how to get to the point. I believe it is a gift from our Creator that we exist. Why we exist is important. That is what spiritually more evolved beings have told me and other people. Is there unique value in humanity? What do you value? Ask yourselves when you are alone. Talk to your loved ones. For me, loving others, doing useful work, learning about our fascinating world, having a good meal, laughing at a funny joke, a good night's sleep, and much more make it worth it. I think Earth is a fine place for humans to live."

The meeting took on a life of its own. George was back to listening and being quiet. The group began searching for ways to save their own lives, their country, and then their focus turned to Asia, Europe, and finally the Americas. President Xi brought the meeting to a close. He asked only that the group continue to keep their minds open until the next meeting in two days.

"Where will you go next, George?"

"My brother promised to tell me soon."

***

Deep in sleep, George was having a bad night. "You can't come here now. So we will come to you." It was Rick. "Here, George, take this old cane pole and come down by the river." It was the deep pool in Northern Spain. Smooth stones, quiet stream, big moon overhead. "Sit down with me, George." The whoosh of bat wings around his head. An owl went "hoooooh." "Look in the pool, George." He stared at the silent ripples and saw a whirlpool. It became wider and deeper. George entered it like on a carnival ride. The whirlpool led him into a room. Someone took his hand and said to follow her. "My name is Margaret." He took her hand. Her eyes were shining and black. Her skin was soft and cool with a color like coffee with cream. "Come with me to this other place." She led him to another door and opened it into a great meeting hall.

There before him, George saw the room was full of shadowy figures of varying degrees of darkness. Margaret said, "These are evil souls returning from Earth. They are without love, selfish, cruel, greedy, and uncaring. Over there is the latest from his failed efforts to escape the Zulus and finally Luiza and Rick. He is a dark soul. These beings are not to be touched. They will be returned to the energy source. They are unteachable. They enter the river of Contempt, and they will cease to exist forever. Before this happens, their life is shown to other souls that may be teachable. It is possible their failure can teach others not to repeat the work of evil."

***

George woke up terrified and in a sweat. "God, what a nightmare." He was still in China, and his mind and bed were a mess. "God, protect us from such evil." He rose from his bed and went to the bathroom. Splashing cold water on his face, he looked in the mirror. "Jesus Christ, calm down. You are okay. You are never going to that place again. Ever!" Later, while eating toast and jelly with a cup of coffee, he heard Rick say, "Hang in there. Good job so far. Next stop, Moscow."

CHAPTER 44

George recalled visiting Russia once before. He had toured Moscow during the early formative years of Yeltsin. He found relative safety in riding the subway, eating in a restaurant, or attending a concert. He took the night train to St. Petersburg and walked the halls of the Hermitage. There were rooms full of original works of the finest European Impressionists and classical sculptures. The poet Pushkin's statues and verse were proudly displayed in the parks of a place no longer called Leningrad. Looking back on this visit twenty years before, he wondered what he was thinking to visit there shortly after a coup. Was the price right? On the night train, a woman was leaving Croatia to escape the Balkan War. She was sharing his berth and was frightened. It didn't help matters that he was an American in deepest Russia. George lent her his Walkman to listen to some soft Brazilian samba music. She calmed right down and went to sleep after that.

George met with President Putin in his Kremlin suite. Apparently, the Chinese President had called ahead, opening the way for the visit. A translator was the only other person present. Hot tea, very dark with lemon, was served with sweet pastries. Little green birds were peeking out around the branches of a maple tree in the garden below.

President Putin knew some English. "Welcome to Russia."

"Spasibo."

Putin mentioned his conversation with President Xi. He was well prepared.

"Please tell me what you have seen."

George said, "I am just a man with some medical experience, and I love science. No one special. The bombings in Tehran and Tel Aviv could trigger further devastation." He told the President of his experiences in Spain and South Africa, including the role of the dark spirits. He described his brother's actions, explaining it was the soul of his deceased brother doing it. He explained what was done by the Zulu warriors and others, including animals, to intervene in the elimination of the dark spirits. "My brother has requested I go and tell important people what I have observed."

The spring sun shone through the window. George found it was soothing and brightened his mind. President Putin noticed the sunlight and smiled.

"Spring is finally here. We are alone because some words are best expressed in private. My political advisors could disturb us were they here. May I call you George?"

"Of course, Sir."

"Last night I had a very odd dream. I am a practical man. Russia has had a brutal history of wars. My purpose has been to lead the country with strength, to restore Russian pride to the people. Now I sound like a politician. I want to prevent the ravages of war from entering our homeland again. The destruction seen recently in the Mideast must be isolated and any spread eliminated.

Now the dream. My mother came to me, and it seemed so real. She was younger—a young, pretty woman. She has been deceased many years. She told me she loved me and was very proud of me. She explained that she was in the after place and what she was doing. She asked me to listen to you. Yes, to you! She said all humans are in the dance together. And then she was gone. What do you think about that?”

“Wow! Do you believe it was really her?”

“Yes, and I feel so good this morning.”

“I know that feeling too. To meet again with a lost loved one. I am a practical man too. I sit here with you. There is fear in my heart for what can be done. I am not sure where I go next or what I must do.”

“Whatever it is, George, I will help you.”

“Thank you, Mr. President.”

A small bird was sitting on the windowsill, peering into the room. A sparrow. In a flash, it took off.

CHAPTER 45 | FRANCE

No message had been delivered yet. George decided to fly to Paris. Something about Russia made him feel uneasy. He did not know that the bombs dropped on Tel Aviv were made in Russia. Others knew this, but was it pertinent? He wasn't even thinking about that. He recalled a pet kitten, Ginger, he had raised. She was a lap cat—short-haired, gray coat with a white star on her chest. She had green eyes and was hyper. She was the lady of the house. One morning, he found her lifeless under a table. She had caught some virus, and the veterinarian had said not to worry about it two days prior. Who said cats were not loving like a dog? George had cried for days after she passed on. He buried her in a field near the railroad track.

The last time he left Moscow was twenty years ago. He had met a beautiful young Russian woman named Svetlana. She was tall, with strawberry blonde hair, bright blue eyes, a cheerful countenance, and spoke very little English. Love like that was not meant to last. She once sent him a box with a pair of her native red shoes in it. It symbolized her intentions to settle with George. It never happened. Both of them found someone else.

***

One summer a decade ago, he visited Paris. Let's see how Paris is in the springtime. It was a clear day, and the French countryside was green. There was a lengthy taxi ride from the airport to a small hotel near the city center. Hotel Genevieve was close to the subway and a lovely park. He thought of going on a tour bus ride. Nah. Be an American in Paris. Look at the flower gardens or visit a museum. Have lunch at a sidewalk café.

The hotel was not a five-star. It was clean and quiet. Settling in, he needed to take a nap. Still no messages. He took a shower and put on fresh clothes. Around the corner, there was a little café. He ordered a coffee and a pastry. The street was almost empty. Was this siesta time? The smell of blossoms was in the air. Birds were singing their hearts out for a possible mate. A few people were coming and going on their way. She was dressed in a pink blouse and a light green skirt. Her eyes were sparkling blue. She had long, straight dirty blonde hair. She smiled at nothing in particular. Her fingers were slender. The nails were crimson. It seemed a good idea to lay down five euros and follow her. She looked like Jane Birkin, but she was not. Her legs were long, and she had rounded hips. He followed her into the park. Little green sprouts were becoming leaves on the trees. Bees bounced from red to purple to yellow flowers. A fountain splashed out a gentle tune. A squirrel hopped, then stopped, his tail twitching neurotically.

She sat down beneath an oak tree on a wooden bench. From her pocket, she produced a piece of bread. Tossing bits out on the path, a robin saw it and flew over to pounce on them.

"Toi aussi, Monsieur écureuil?"

The squirrel came scampering over for his share. On another bench not too far away, George sat down and watched. Without thinking, he said, "What about me?"

Smiling, she tossed a piece of bread at him.

"Bonjour, merci beaucoup. Belle journée."

"Oui, ça l'est."

"Je m'appelle George."

"Je suis Marie. Do you speak English?"

"Oui, mais juste un peu."

"George, do you know Luiza?"

"Yes, I know a Luiza. She was with my brother. How do you know her?"

She walked over to him.

"May I sit here?"

"Yes, of course."

"Let me try to explain myself. I am an actress with some popularity here in my native France. Last night, after a long day of rehearsals and some takes on the set for a film, I went home. I was tired and ate a light supper. Then I took a relaxing bath and went to bed. After several hours of restful sleep, I had a dream.

In this dream, a woman named Luiza came to me and invited me to visit a garden with her. She took my hand, and we were in a jungle of plants and birds and bugs. We walked a short distance to a clearing with fresh smells of flowers and sunlight radiating through the treetops. We sat on a log near a quiet little stream.

Luiza described herself to me. She told me of living in this forest as a native and later being adopted by a European woman. She told me about visiting the garden for its peace and serenity. Her eyes glowed with intense light. She was dressed as a native tribal woman. She asked me to contact you with a message."

George was listening carefully and with great interest.

"Marie, please tell me what the message was."

"She wanted me to accompany you to America when you go there to speak to the president. I don't know what this is about or why you are going there. She said you will know."

He was perplexed about how he just happened to follow this lovely woman into the park.

"Luiza must have described me to you. Otherwise, how would you know to speak with me here?"

Marie said, "I saw you in my dream. I saw us speaking as we are right now on this park bench."

"Oh, I understand now. Well, do you want to go with me to America and speak to the president?"

"Merci beaucoup. Yes, please."

George was lost in the eyes of this beautiful woman. Her eyes were dark and bright. Her face was slender, and she had a straight nose. Her hair was blonde and flew in the breeze. She had just a touch of red lipstick and a gap in the middle of her top front teeth. Her English with a French accent was very pleasant to hear. Her voice was clear, smooth, and sweet. And loud. The voice projected like a well-tuned musical instrument.

She handed him a card with her full name and address. Her phone number was handwritten on the back. He saw her last name was Angelle.

"I will call you soon, Marie. Merci. Bonjour."

"Merci, George. Je l'attendrai impatiemment."

***

Something was not right. George sensed a fly in the ointment or a pebble in his shoe. A good sense of smell and proven diagnostic skill convinced George to sleep on it. He would call Marie in the morning. She had a natural beauty and charm, like a diamond in the rough. There was something in his mind like a little red light. He used to drive a Mercedes with one hundred forty thousand miles on it. A "check engine" light would come on frequently. At first it worried him until he learned it was the computer. When he rebooted the computer, the light would go off. The car ran well either way.

Back in the Hotel Genevieve, the day had gone well. He found a few moments to kneel beside the bed and pray. "I offer myself to

Thee to use me and to build with me as Thou wilt. Relieve me of the bondage of self, that I may do Thy will. Take away my difficulties, that victory over them may bear witness to others I may help of Thy love, Thy power, and Thy way of life. May I do Thy will always."

A deep sleep was provided. At some point, a dream began. His mother was there, which often led to some disturbance. This time she was calm and patient. "George, I love you. I am proud of your work and efforts to help people on earth. I have had some valuable guidance and healing here in my spiritual home. Though I was often a source of turmoil to you and others when I was there, I am making amends. Do you trust me enough to listen to me?"

"Yes, and I still love you, Mom."

She continued, "I have some information from Ricky and Luiza. Marie is a lovely woman, as you must have noticed. She is a gifted actress. Both Ricky and Luiza have asked me to tell you this. They are aware of an unknown entity that has been manipulating her. There is concern the entity is evil. Though I am only learning about this gradually, there is more I must learn about evil. It is outside the will and love of God. I do not understand much of this yet. As I come to you as your mother, it is with my love for you. You must learn more of what she is doing and why. Have courage and trust in God."

He sensed a hug and a kiss from her, and then she was gone. He slept well after that.

***

Over coffee and a croissant, George looked at the card. "Mme Marie Angelle, Delacroix 19, suite 2, Paris." The phone was a local landline. He decided to call her now. She answered on the third ring.

"Bonjour?"

"Hello, this is George calling. Is this Marie?"

"Oh yes. Well, hello. How are you today?"

"I am fine, thanks. And you?"

"Just fine, thanks."

"Marie, I wondered if you might meet me for dinner tonight? I want to talk with you about the trip and some thoughts in mind as we prepare our journey overseas."

Marie was receptive and knew a place to meet for supper called the Beaurenaud near the Quai de Montebello. He would pick her up by taxi around eight. George found her voice cheerful. No hint of malice there.

CHAPTER 46 | FRANCE

They had roast duck, and it was delicious. There were small roasted potatoes with asparagus and cream sauce. George was not a connoisseur of food or wine. He knew his appetite was well satisfied. Marie was oh so pretty. She wore a red dress that suggested her bohemian appeal. Simple and not too revealing. She had a wonderful figure, which anyone could see. She wore emerald earrings, which George found distracting to his attention on her dark blue eyes. So far, he could find no trace of some hidden agenda in Marie.

"Tell me, Marie, has anyone besides Luiza spoken to you in a dream? I mean about our trip overseas. Or possibly anyone else outside of the dream?"

"This all seems very strange to me. I have been uncertain with all of this. Before Luiza spoke to me in the garden, my life was not going well. My partner had found another woman. Of course, my work has been satisfying. More work awaits me when I return from our visit to America. I have a child who is ten. His name is Philippe. My mother will care for him while I am away. He is a good boy. Quite truthfully, I have been a little depressed with my personal life. That is all I can think of. What else are you concerned about?"

"Marie, the world is in turmoil over the bombings. This is a very dangerous time. I have been helped by my brother Rick and by Luiza. They have encouraged me to go and visit places to assist in stopping further destruction. What I have learned convinces me there exist some dark—yes, evil—beings actively causing more fear and hatred in people. My faith in a loving, divine God keeps me going. There are loved ones and friends in spirit helping me too.”

“What do you mean by evil beings? What can you tell me?”

The waiter came over to serve more coffee. They paused and got more hot coffee. George did not want to go into the whole history of Spain and South Africa. He chose to mention the evidence for something evil there and the connection it had with the nuclear tragedies. “Something evil continues to mess with human beings trying to make their way forward. Why it is, given our Creator could put an end to it, is a mystery to me. I know some loving power has probably carried me away from death’s door before. It strikes me as a serious struggle happening on earth, and we are all in it.”

“Oui, I understand only a little of this. Something has happened lately that may be useful. There has been someone or something around me at times. It is, how do you say it, a woman’s intuition? Maybe not real. Someone may be following me. My mother worries about me and Philippe. She asks me what is wrong. Even in this lovely restaurant, it is like a scene in a play where some dialogue or prop is out of place.” She looked around to observe who was there. An older, well-dressed man could be seen dining with an elegant younger lady. Marie stared at him momentarily. George followed her gaze.

“Is there somebody there you know, Marie?”

"That man is familiar. Yes, I saw him at the market a few days ago. He was looking at me that day and turned away when I saw him. I feel uncomfortable now. Could we go?"

"Yes, let's go."

They strolled along the river Seine. There was a full moon. The air was clear and dry. The street lamps glowed softly like a Van Gogh painting. They came to a bridge and walked across it. A long tour boat full of gaping or smiling passengers passed beneath them. George held Marie's arm, and when he realized it, he released it, saying, "Sorry." Marie smiled and said, "That's fine. No apology necessary." She put her arm around his.

Somewhere in the distance, the well-dressed gentleman was observing them. His eyes were sharp and focused like a hawk. The sight of her arm in his made him pause. He smiled. He was alone. Off in the further distance, peering from a tower of Notre Dame, was the free spirit of Rick. He was not alone. Luiza was with him.

The taxi returned Marie with George to her home. She kissed him on the cheek. She promised to be ready for their departure to the airport in the morning. She made her way safely to her door and entered. George gave the driver his address, and away they went.

CHAPTER 47 | FRANCE

The world was in a surreal parody of normalcy since the last bombing. A man and woman could take a pleasant walk in a Paris park. A pregnant woman on a Chicago bus was having early contractions on her ride home. The fringes of Tehran were still smoldering while stunned, grieving survivors wandered around the rubble. Little progress had been made in cleaning up the devastation of Tel Aviv.

A world war was imminent. The outcry for the elimination of all of Israel was heard from the entire Muslim world. Israel could barely restrain the cries for total military victory over all Muslim targets. The leaders of all the major world powers conversed by direct hotlines. A consensus was gradually reached.

The world powers were going to hold a summit meeting. The last Nuclear Security Summit was held in Washington, D.C., in April of that year. For reasons of expedience, the same location was to be used that week. The attendees were different this time. In addition to political and military leaders, various spiritual leaders, psychologists, and philosophers would be included. The nature of the conflict struck at the very heart of humanity. The question each attendee was asked before coming was: how can we learn to live together safely and stop the mass destruction?

Some of those invited were not politically correct. For example, tribal leaders from Africa and the Pacific Islands, or a witch doctor from a Native Indian tribe, were included. As the details of the reservations were revealed, administrators and journalists were scratching their heads. Some said it looked like an odd bunch of carnival clowns. What did they have to do with world peace (or war)?

***

That night Marie had a visitor while deep asleep in her bed. It was the well-dressed gentleman. His name was Lucifer. His message was delivered to her on a subconscious level. For some days, he had softly entered her mind. Having presented himself as a guardian and friend, he now had her confidence. He resembled her grandfather on her mother's side. She had a special affection for him.

Lucifer had been patrolling the inhabitants of Earth for hundreds of years. He was full of resentment and hatred. He despised all things good. His purpose in life was to upset harmony and happiness in all manner of life on Earth. Once upon a time, long ago, the spirit of Lucifer never got the love and respect he thought he deserved. He was special and different. He was so different that he was going to become a new and bold spirit. He used free choice selfishly. His spirit used humans to defeat them and make his own reign on Earth.

Lucifer began his suggestions to Marie. "You are beautiful. Men find you attractive. They feel like horny teenagers around you. George likes your type and wants you. George has his own special desires. Let me share with you what he wants in a woman." So he told her.

Their flight to America went smoothly. They were taken to a four-star hotel not far from Dulles Airport. They had separate rooms. Marie said she wanted to order room service. "Please join me, George, so we can talk about our plans for tomorrow." George hesitated as they made their way to the elevator. It was late for supper, and he wanted to relax then get some sleep. He agreed to join her in her room in about an hour. He found her sexy even after the very long flight. She smiled, showing him that gap in her front teeth. Her eyes sparkled. It was like music to hear her speak English with a French accent.

For reasons she couldn't fully explain, Marie found George desirable. She somehow knew what he would enjoy in bed. *How do I know his fantasies?* she wondered. She recalled catching him admiring her butt and thighs—despite always wearing slacks when flying. *I'll take a thorough shower and then order our meals,* she decided. But how did she even know he liked her scent? The fragrance of her body?

Stripping down to her lingerie, she studied herself in the mirror. She still had it. Turning around, she examined her backside—smooth, pale, unblemished. Satisfied, she stepped into the shower.

Meanwhile, George was shaving, peering into his own eyes—brown, with hints of green. *Remember why you're here. Think with your big head, not the little one.* A tune popped into his mind—

Donna Summer's "I Feel Love." *No, George. Not that kind of love. Take your shower.*

He knocked. Marie opened the door, smiling. She smelled of spring-fresh citrus blossoms.

"Come in, have a seat. Want a drink?"

"I haven't touched alcohol in years. Got a diet soda?"

"Sure," she said, heading off. She wore a simple pastel house dress—short hem, barefoot, no stockings.

Is this a conflict of interest? George wondered. *Focus. Eat supper. Talk about the meeting.*

"I ordered broiled mahi-mahi with a baked potato and salad. That okay?"

"Perfect. One of my favorites."

She handed him the drink. Her fingers were long and slender, nails painted bright red.

"Remind me—who'll be at the meeting?"

"All the major political powers and top military brass. France will be there. The U.S. President with his advisors. And interestingly—key religious leaders, psychologists, philosophers, even a few shamans."

Marie leaned forward, cleavage exposed, reaching for a napkin.

"Tell me more about those religious folks."

"Word is, the Pope, the Dalai Lama, Muslim clerics, Protestant ministers, Jewish rabbis, and spiritual leaders from Africa, the Pacific, and South America. Some scientists and philosophers, too."

"That's a strange mix. Won't it just complicate everything?"

"A valid point. But I'm following instructions."

She leaned forward again, baring her breasts. George caught the scent of her perfume. Their eyes met—hers sincere, with a faint glow of desire. She was irresistible. Despite prior warnings about her, he looked—unapologetically—at her bare chest. Her pink nipples stood out. He wanted to touch her, kiss her, hold her.

"Room service," came a voice.

"That must be supper," she said.

They ate quietly. Afterward, George leaned back, full but distracted. Passion lingered just beneath the surface. Then—*the meeting,* he reminded himself.

"Marie, have you experienced anything unusual lately? Strange dreams? Odd encounters?"

She looked surprised.

"What does that have to do with tomorrow's meeting?"

"Everything. Remember that man in Paris? Think carefully—any disturbing dreams? Emotions upon waking that didn't belong to you?"

"No monsters or nightmares," she said. "Nothing scary." But she blushed, knowing what George desired in her—and in bed. She couldn't explain how, but she *knew*.

"Let me be blunt," George said. "I don't know you well, but I believe you're a good person. Still, trusted sources tell me someone may be manipulating you. It can happen without your awareness. Use fear as a warning. Trust your instincts. I'll share experiences tomorrow that affect all humanity. But I must check my own motives, too. We're all part of something bigger."

Marie nodded slowly. "Some roles I've played turned out more important than I first realized. I get that. But being a pawn? I hate that. I'll search my memories—use my detective instincts to sniff out anything off."

She stood, covering her neckline with her hand. "I'm tired. I need to sleep."

George agreed. "Good night."

That night, in deep sleep, Marie was visited again by Lucifer. But she was harder to reach now. He could no longer implant thoughts or memories with ease. *Someone has warned her,* he realized. *No matter. I've dealt with resistance before. Pride and vanity will work.*

He began to flatter her.

You are lovely, Marie—irresistible. Your femininity turns men into eager adolescents. Your eyes, your smile—radiant with warmth. Your intellect and spiritual strength will lead to power. Find a powerful man. Gain his trust.

Lucifer wasn't done. He had other pawns.

There was the Russian General Dyumin—defiant, skeptical, unwilling to play anyone's game. Lucifer had visited him, too.

Then there was General Chang in China, ready to act on Lucifer's command. And there were others—fanatical Zionists, Islamists, and Christians—all useful for fueling hatred. This war would consume civilization. And Lucifer would seize control.

Somehow, it would happen.

CHAPTER 48 | Washington, D.C., USA

George was deeply impressed with Marie's cheerful confidence. She was as pretty as a princess and as sexy as a beauty queen.

"Hello, Marie. You're looking just fine."

They got into a limousine provided by the American President.

"Thank you, George. I hope I am ready to meet with so many dignitaries. Being an actress, one may think I am immune to stage fright. Not so. They say practice makes perfect."

They drove along in silence, taking in the sights of the Lincoln Monument and later Arlington National Cemetery.

"Someone or something came into my sleep last night."

George turned to look at her.

"When I woke this morning, I lay still and searched inside my mind. I feel wonderful, full of self-confidence. I looked in the mirror and became very satisfied with myself. I haven't felt this good in over a year. Like being in love again. You wanted me to look inside, didn't you, George?"

"Yes, I did. What makes you think someone may have visited you in your sleep?"

"It may be my instincts. There is no memory of anyone. When I act in a play, the writer and director tell me how to be. Then I can make believe. It is what I do. The character I play is someone else and I become that person. There is awareness of what the author wants. It is like that now and why I say there may possibly have been a presence in my mind last night."

George paused, thinking. Say a prayer with her.

"Marie, will you pray with me?"

She said yes.

"With thanks, we offer our gratitude for the many blessings we receive. Guide us, Lord, as we speak and act on Your behalf today. Help us to do Your will for the good of all."

"Marie, the sense of being visited by someone last night I believe to be important. As we arrive at the meeting now, more signals or insights may arise. Refrain from reacting impulsively. Come to me if you are unsure or if you become aware of more important concerns."

She said she will try.

***

They were escorted to a secure location, passing armed guards three times. Eventually, they arrived at a spacious office where they met the American President, who was accompanied by a small group of dignitaries. He began by expressing his anxiety and fear about current world events.

"I have spoken to and listened to many world leaders, including the Russian and Chinese Presidents. They will be here today. They mentioned strange personal stories about their deceased mother or father meeting with them in a dream. Personally, I have not had any such unusual events occur."

The President looked at Marie and became aware of a stirring inside. The President began to stare at her eyes. He appeared captivated by her presence. He began to speak, then saw her bosom under her dress. He shuffled a bit and looked at her hands. The feeling was like a seventeen-year-old boy in heat for his secret love.

An aide intervened, "Mr. President?"

As though being caught by the head schoolmaster in a naughty daydream (which he was), he became flushed and startled.

"Oh yes. Sorry, I was just thinking about something, uh, where was I?"

He couldn't help it. He looked back at Marie and she smiled back at him. He felt that stirring in his loins again. Marie actually looked down at his crotch and smiled again.

The President asked the others to excuse them while he met with Marie and George privately. They all stood up and left the room.

George was wondering what was going on. The President stood up, revealing there was an obvious development in his pants. He turned away and used his hand to adjust the inconvenient evidence. Marie didn't miss a thing. Neither did George.

"Would you like a coffee or a drink?"

Marie chose juice. George found a cold bottle of water. The President chose water too.

"Now, where were we? Oh yeah. George, can you confirm the reports I've gotten that ghosts or spirits have visited world dignitaries are true?"

"Whoever has communicated with them I cannot know in fact," said George. "I have been contacted directly by my brother, who died about 50 years ago. I was present to observe the elimination of an evil being in Spain and one in South Africa. These things are true. I am here to tell you and the others here about it."

The President was distracted by Marie. His face was flushed. His eyes were on her face and figure.

"This all sounds very bizarre. Like we are on some witch hunt. The media and American people are going to think I'm losing it. It will bring me and the government scorn. Why frighten people about what may be some isolated bad guys? It sounds like voodoo. People fear the unknown."

George sat in silence. Then said, "There are more than two million dead in the Mideast. Is that voodoo?"

"Well no, it is not. It is a tragedy. Are you so sure there is this connection with evil and the crimes against humanity we see? And if so, what do you suggest we do about it?"

"Personally, I am convinced. Not only of these recent catastrophes, but of the likelihood of more to come."

Marie stirred in her chair.

"Perhaps it is best if I excuse myself and let you speak alone. Please excuse me."

She rose and left, closing the door behind her.

"She is a lovely woman. Why is she here? Is she your lady friend, George?"

The President was disappointed by her exit.

"I met her in a park in Paris. She is an actress and not my girlfriend. Her presence has meant to me more of companionship. The past few weeks have been confusing and unsettling. I've felt anxious and unsure. She offered to accompany me, and her presence is reassuring—nothing more. She's a kind person with good intentions. I hope she hasn't been a bother to you."

"No, not at all. On the contrary, she is quite an eyeful. That is not like me to be drawn to a woman so readily. Did you notice?"

"Well, yes, Mr. President."

"Hmm! Not very diplomatic of me. Hah! Hell, I'm a father and I have a daughter about her age. My thoughts are better kept to the serious issue at hand. So tell me a little more now. Is it Dr. Elliott or do you prefer George?"

"George is fine. One concern comes through to me. Whether one believes in humans having souls that live on after the veil of death, the world as we know it is having serious problems. It is sick. The powers that be can work together to prevent a total train wreck.

The earth is beautiful and it can be salvaged and repaired. Humans can make that happen."

"I like that, George. It is practical. Shall we go out there now?"

"Yes, Mr. President."

CHAPTER 49

Does anyone feel sorry for those that take pleasure in knowingly causing great harm, even death, to others? To harm wantonly the plants, animals, humans, and earth? Who cares for those that do that? Some of these tainted souls were still loved by their mothers.

Lucifer walked among the crowd awaiting the entrance of the President and the other dignitaries. He was dressed in clerical robes without any given type or distinction. His white beard gave him that wise old man look. There were military uniforms in abundance. Politicians from every corner were shaking hands and meeting once again. Spiritual healers, religious leaders, and tribal chiefs sampled the refreshments and tried to exchange salutations.

A famous medicine man named Boa from the South Pacific Island Balboa was wearing a sharp Italian suit. He was speaking to a Sunni Muslim Imam from Fallujah.

"My friend, how can we find some peaceful solution to man's instincts gone wild?"

"That is the problem, Boa. I must agree. The answer is not war and bombs. What do you think?"

"The island people would gather and pray to call upon the spirits of their ancestors. The women would prepare a feast and offer it to the people of the enemy. I have seen this work. Also, the women would gather and decide to stop having relations with their warrior men. The men did not fight well after this. They became grumpy and irritable. So they listened to their women, who said, 'find better ways to settle your differences.' Competitions were held for wrestling and throwing boomerangs. Exchanging jokes over the campfires that cooked fresh fish and vegetables with fruits for a feast often had the angry ones laughing."

The Sunni man smiled.

"I wonder if that would work? Our ancestors were fond of gathering in the desert for a feast too. There was music and horse racing. The strongest young men would wrestle and often forget why they wanted to kill one another. The women would sing and dance and exchange clothing and jewelry. The children never cared about the reason for fighting when they played."

Lucifer was creeping about. "I'll be damned if these idiots ever find peace of mind and satisfaction. Having feasts with your enemies and children playing, bah!" He had found his mark. It was often necessary to stir the soup and boil the broth. The meeting hall was more of an auditorium. Flags from every nation were draped along the walls. Lucifer told the Imam from Iraq that an Israeli rabbi had said the Sunni Muslims were all liars and thieves, and that the Iraqi flag was ugly and filthy. The Imam became enraged. He jumped up and down, made fists, and yelled some obscenity. He took off his shoe and threw it at the Israeli flag, screaming, "Allahu Akbar." The Israeli rabbi saw this and, with murder in his mind, ran at the Imam wildly, screaming his righteous indignation. He smashed into him like a linebacker. He cold-cocked the Imam, and they both crashed to the floor in a flurry of robes and caps.

"Now we're getting somewhere," said Lucifer. They were trying to strangle each other. The security guards pounced on the tangled bodies and pulled them apart. Profanity and wild punches were thrown about. Soon others were joining in the ruckus. A Buddhist priest lost composure and struck a Chinese politician without warning. A fat U.S. Army general tripped a Russian general, and then all hell broke loose. An Asian Indian colonel screamed and dove on a Pakistani officer. The Venezuelan President struck the Spanish King on the nose, yelling, "Cállate tu boca, hijo de puta!" Food was flying around the room. A lemon pie smashed into the Japanese President's face. A Maori tribal chief punched the Anglican priest in the belly. A devout middle-aged nun got into the spirit of things by delivering a full-face slap to a Wiccan priestess.

Lucifer went skulking like a crusty crab into the shadows of the hall. It was all so much fun, and he chuckled. "Look at those stupid monkeys. I wonder where Marie is?" Searching the chaos around him, he could see her seated near the stage beside General Chang. She had a shocked expression on her face. Lucifer whispered, "Your beauty makes grown men act like lust-filled teenage boys."

The general began staring at her. He touched her hand. Marie looked at him and saw his eyes bulging out intensely. She was not surprised. She had seen this before. She smiled at the man. He became bolder and said, "Let's go somewhere else. It is not safe here." He put his arm around her and headed for the next exit. Marie sensed the script had now changed, like a dream that suddenly and mysteriously changes scenes. Lucifer was now writer and director.

The general scurried away with Marie in tow. He was searching for a private room. Down the hallway, he found a door labeled "Utility Room." They entered it and saw glowing lights on panel boxes on the wall. He turned on the light and saw how pretty she was. He was like a kid again, ready to do anything to satisfy his lust.

Marie noticed the bulge in his pants. He kissed her on the lips. She was receptive, pushing back with her tongue in his mouth. She yielded her hips into his. He moaned and hugged her tighter. His hands lowered down to squeeze her bottom. He was like a stallion in heat.

"General, should we be doing this?"

In response, he said, "I think I love you. You are my princess."

She said, "There is something you should know. While I was in the office with the President and George, I heard them saying China may be the real culprit. The President had a plan to disgrace China and advance his own agenda."

This struck General Chang like a bucket of ice water in the face. "I knew it. I told President Xi this same thing."

Marie kept it going. "It would upset the world balance of power. Others must be warned."

The general was torn now between his love of China and his raging hormones. He decided to take matters into his own hands. Marie felt his hand upon her breast and gasped. She was keenly aware of his stiffened loins pushing against her. She pushed him back and dropped down to unbuckle his belt and pull his pants down. His underwear was sticking out at attention. The briefs had the panda symbol neatly placed on the front.

"How cute," she said. She pulled his briefs down, and out popped his dong. Marie was ready to give it a big kiss when the door swung open. It was the U.S. President, who said, "You little prick!"

George was behind a Secret Service agent at the door. He peeked into the room. General Chang's eyes were glazed and shining like a startled bull in heat. Marie was dumbstruck, yet somehow smiling like a little girl caught with her hand in the cookie jar.

George said, "Mr. President, think of your wife, your daughter, and your supporters."

The President looked down at the floor. He mumbled, "Excuse us. Let's get out of here."

The President turned and left. The door closed behind him. General Chang looked at his privates, which were in fast retreat from their state of readiness. He pulled his pants up, buckled his belt, and staggered out of the room. Before the door closed completely, George entered the room.

"Marie, Marie? Are you OK? What happened? Marie, are you listening?"

She looked at George with a blank expression. "What?"

"Are you okay, Marie?"

She said, "I don't really know. Was I about to do oral sex on him?"

"It looked that way."

She began to gasp, then cry. George came over to her and took her arm, raising her up. "We can go outside and sit there."

They left the room and returned to the main hall. They found a place removed from the crowd and sat down. Marie began to sob, so George found a tissue for her. She grew quiet.

"I said something to the general. It is very important I remember what it was."

"I'm listening, Marie. Do you mean before we opened the door?"

"Yes, it must have been before. I remember the sense of acting in a part with a new writer and director. The setting and tone were different. Do you know what I mean?"

"Yes, I think I do."

Marie said, "Just before General Chang and I went to that room, the tone had changed. I began saying and doing things that were not my own."

"What did you say to the General?"

"I said the U.S. planned to blame and then disgrace China for the Mideast bombings so the U.S. could gain power. The general was convinced it was true. It's not true, is it? Oh my God, what have I done?"

"No, it's not true. We have to speak to the U.S. President and the Chinese to convince them it's not true. Let's get going. I will be speaking to everyone soon."

CHAPTER 50 | Washington, D.C., USA

They made their way through the auditorium.

"Have you seen anyone like that well-dressed man in Paris? How about unusual thoughts or hearing a voice?"

"Whether it was a voice or thought, I am not sure. About the same time the script changed, I recall a message that said I was so beautiful that grown men acted like horny teenagers around me."

"That may be him. He may be here and using you and others. Let me go tell the President and get ready for the presentation."

Marie said, "What can I do? I am ashamed and frightened."

"Marie, you are here for a reason. Try to stay strong. Do you have faith in God or a superior power?"

"Yes, I pray to Mother Mary. I was raised Catholic."

George said, "Say a prayer to your guardian spirit that you love and trust. She will surely listen to you. Don't let that liar get to you. Tell it to leave. I must go and speak to the President now."

As George made his way across the auditorium, Lucifer saw him.

"That guy is a troublemaker. He is up to something. I will send him a surprise."

Then he saw the Russian General Dyumin.

"Now there is a man willing to do what is necessary."

The Russian General did not trust this spiritual bullshit. He trusted boots on the ground, superior strength, and good reconnaissance.

General Dyumin saw Marie looking upset. He stopped to introduce himself.

"My name is General Dyumin. Are you all right, madame? You appear upset."

Lucifer saw this encounter.

"Remember, Marie, you are so beautiful that grown men love you like boys in heat."

Alarms were going off in her head.

"Mother Mary, the angel of protection, I beseech thee in my shame and moment of need. Help me, please."

Lucifer observed her weeping and distraught.

"Hmm. She is not reacting as before. She seems to be praying. Shit!"

"I said, are you all right? Can I help you? As a gentleman, I offer my assistance to you."

Marie looked up. "What?"

She heard the voice again, "You are so beautiful." Her eyes flashed and she blushed. A glow came over her. She smiled at the

General. He was stunned by her change. He thought, *What a lovely woman.*

"My name is General Dyumin. Who are you?"

"My name is Marie, and I am visiting from France. Are you a Russian officer?"

"Yes, I am a General in the Russian Army."

"Yes, you are," cooed Marie.

The General straightened up and smiled.

"I don't want to sound forward, but your bouquet aroma is entrancing."

She said, "I am not wearing perfume. It is my natural scent, perhaps."

He said, "It reminds me of nature and wheat during the harvest."

"Oh, how romantic, General," said Marie.

He continued, "May I sit down with you here?"

"Yes, please do."

He sat down next to Marie. His eyes were alight with playful passion for this intoxicatingly lovely woman. He recalled similar passion when he was about twenty and in the military university in Moscow. The girls loved him in uniform. Now, a grown officer, married with three married daughters of his own, he was delighted to feel young and dashing again.

Marie smiled and touched his hand.

"Thank you for joining me. I was distraught. So much has been happening, and so quickly. My mind was in a spin."

She felt compelled to speak about the CIA plans.

"It frightens me to say this, but I overheard the US President tell someone in his office about a plan to blame Russia for starting the war between Israel and Iran. He wants to discredit Russia so the United States will have more power."

"Chyort! That's what I suspected. All this talk about spiritual beings and changing our beliefs is a trick. I saw you talking with General Chang. Did he say anything about this?"

"He is convinced it is a trick too. He ran off to tell his President of the deception just before I met here with you."

General Dyumin stood up.

"Please excuse me, Marie. I have to go speak to my President to tell him the same thing. Perhaps we can meet again later when all these dangerous lies are revealed and order is restored."

She gave him her hand, he kissed it, and ran off. In Marie's mind she heard, "You are so beautiful." But she did not feel beautiful. She felt confused and disturbed. She felt shame and guilt. It was a feeling of having betrayed her true nature, her son, her family, and the God of her understanding. She considered harming herself.

She went to the terrace. She could see a courtyard some thirty feet below. Her self-disgust and guilt made her want to throw herself out the window. She lowered her head and prayed silently. She asked for forgiveness and assistance in releasing her from this evil hold on her. In her mind she was told to go down the stairs and meet with the lady waiting down below. She did not see a lady down there. She proceeded as told.

She went down the stairs and then saw a lady sitting in the courtyard. It was dark, but the woman had a faint light glow around her. The lady looked up, and her eyes were dark and shone like a nocturnal animal of the forest. She tapped on the bench beside her and waved Marie to come over. Marie looked closely and knew she must sit down beside this woman. She held her head down and walked to the bench. She crossed herself and actually kneeled down before the bench. She was crying softly and saw a teardrop hit the lady's black shoe. This was not a dream, though she wondered if she was going insane.

The hand of the woman lifted Marie's head up to face her. The woman smiled and said, "Here, sit beside me." Marie did.

"My name is Luiza. I visited you once before while you were asleep in Paris. The elder spirits understand your request. I have come to help you. You are an actress, aren't you?"

"Yes, that is my profession."

"Have you some idea that your acting skills have been under the direction of some evil being?"

"George has spoken with me about this. Why is someone trying to use me?"

Luiza continued, "I know George, and he knows of me. We both know his brother Rick. Has George told you about us?"

"Yes, he has. He has been concerned that someone is using me or trying to reach me in my dreams. What is going on? I am going crazy over all of this."

Luiza placed her softly glowing arm around Marie.

"You are being used by a very bad director. He is called Lucifer. You are a good person, and no, you are not crazy."

Marie began to feel immediate relief. The love of forgiveness. She cried and hugged Luiza.

"Thank you, Luiza."

The soft blue glow enveloped Marie, and she became aware of a peace beyond all misunderstanding.

"Go and speak to the Russian and Chinese Generals. Explain to them the truth."

And then Luiza was gone. She looked for Luiza but could not find her. Marie made her way back up the stairs to the auditorium. She went directly to the Russian dignitaries at their table. She saw General Dyumin speaking to his President. Before she could approach, a guard stopped her. The Russian General told the guard to allow her to come forward.

"I apologize if I am interrupting you here. I want to share with you what I have just learned. General Dyumin, what I told you was not true. The American President did not plan a trick or betrayal. He did not say he would blame Russia for the disasters in the Mideast. You must believe me now."

"First you admit to lying to me, and now you would have us believe you. Explain yourself."

"There is somebody manipulating me, or was manipulating me. The passion we felt was brought about by some evil coercion. I don't know how, but it is sinister."

Before the General could respond, the President intervened.

"Why are you telling us this now?"

She responded, "I was met by a woman in the courtyard just now. She said her name was Luiza. I believe she came from beyond our physical world. She told me an evil one is directing me to cause us all harm. Her love was perfect, like I have received from my own mother."

"Spaseeba. That is what I know too. My own mother came to me in my sleep before Dr. Elliott spoke to us about the spirits in our meeting in Moscow. It is why I am here and now believe Marie is telling the truth. What else can you tell us, Marie?"

General Dyumin was about to speak about that "spirit crap," but President Putin silenced him.

"I told General Chang the same thing—that the Americans were using a clandestine plot to trick them. I must find General Chang and stop him."

"It may be too late for that," said General Dyumin. "I spoke to him just a while ago and saw him running off to warn his people."

"Where is my direct line phone?" said the President. "I must reach them quickly."

The security men were not prepared for that question. They were looking at each other in confusion.

A huge explosion was heard coming from the far end of the auditorium—the same area the American President had his office.

CHAPTER 51 | Washington, D.C., USA

Hard lessons. Brothers and sisters don't weep. Beware the friends you keep.

There was gray-black smoke roiling into the hall from the blast. People were on the floor, under tables and chairs, screams all about. A thousand times before and a thousand times more. Somewhere in the gloom, Lucifer was humming a tune. And humans had crawled from the sea into the swamp. Over eons, man has grown. They have evolved into their own. In their souls are found hard lessons learned. Got to grow up our spirits to keep. Like turn the other cheek.

The President of the United States had died in the blast. George was under the rubble in another room, unconscious but not alone. Once again, his brother and friend had protected him. He whispered into George's mind, "Time to get up, George. I have my eye out for that little shit. So go out now. Tell them why you are here. The power of God's love is beyond all fear and misunderstanding. I will keep your back."

"OK, Rick."

George arose and fumbled in the dark. He made his way through the rubble and out of the room.

Marie was on the floor. Luiza whispered in her ear, "The Chinese are over there. Tell them the truth."

CHAPTER 52

The blast area was secured, and FBI specialists were collecting evidence. The crowd of attendees was not allowed to leave. They were settled in the main hall awaiting an announcement from the acting President. The Vice President asked all to be patient as the crime scene was worked. She wanted the audience to listen as she offered up her respects. The body of the President was taken to the medical examiner at Walter Reed Medical Center.

The Vice President said the President had died from the bomb blast. Details of the crime scene and security cameras were under review. She asked the close friend of the President, the Secretary of Defense, to come forward and share a few words. The Secretary of Defense was by his side when he died.

"For all of us who knew him as a friend and a great leader, and to his wife and family, I offer my deepest sympathies. The President gave me a brief message before he died. He said, 'Tell my wife and children I love them. Though I am dying before you, my spirit is alive and well. There is a new home that awaits me now. I know this because my grandmother is here and just said, "Oh come on, boy."' He asked that the meeting go forward too."

Since they could not leave immediately, George was asked to give his talk.

"Does it matter who started the war in the Middle East? Who or what killed the President tonight? Yes, it does. It is known by me and many others that our human spirits, our souls, live on after we physically die. My deceased brother has met with me many times since he died many years ago. Even tonight, he told me to get up off the floor and speak with you. The one who placed the bomb assassinating the President is here now."

Lucifer enjoyed the attention. There was a gleam in his hate-filled eyes. He was proud. He was powerful and deserved respect. Dressed in a red robe as a medieval shaman, the urge to kill some more grew. He had seen Msizi in the audience. Lucifer felt the oldest reason for killing a man: revenge. He reasoned that Msizi had brought destruction to some of his allies. "Kill him before he kills you," he whispered to himself. He had a stiletto up his sleeve.

Moving up behind Msizi, he prepared to strike. His arm came up with the dagger poised to plunge deep into his back. At that moment, a tremendous blow was delivered by a fist into Lucifer's chest. Rick watched him collapse like a puppet with his strings cut. Rick stepped on the hand holding the knife. He grabbed the knife and handed it to Msizi. Rick said, "He was going to stab you with this."

Rick grabbed Lucifer around the waist and stood him up. He pulled the hood off his head to reveal the face. Rick said, "This is the one who bombed the President and was trying to stab Msizi now." Lucifer began to resist, but Rick held his arm with a vise grip. Lucifer began to speak.

"Don't you see? This is the one who killed the President. He has killed before, and he wants to turn us against one another."

Rick smashed his fist into Lucifer's face. "Shut up!" Rick dragged him to the stage, and then several Zulu warriors came forward. Rick asked them to secure him.

"My name is Rick. My brother here is George. I have been instructed to come to the physical world here. My elder spirits want to help people get through this mess without more self-destruction. Please listen to George."

"God, what can I say? You said it all, Rick. I love you and respect you for all you've done. You are courageous, and this is your 'hands-on' way."

Over to the side, Luiza could be seen moving closer. Marie looked up and smiled. Pointing, she said, "That's Luiza from the courtyard. She told me this Lucifer has been the one manipulating me and telling the lies. Is this him?"

Rick said, "Yes."

Lucifer roared, "Get away from me!" He threw his arms up, casting off the Zulus. His eyes were ablaze. "You are all fools! I am free. A free and powerful spirit. I am proud to say I killed the President. Your so-called God is the ultimate slave master. Was he there for you when your child died? Did he care about you when your dreams in life were dashed? Where was he when Hiroshima burned? Why doesn't he just clean up the air and the seas? The poor get poorer and the rich get richer. Fuck him!"

George asked him, "What happened to you? Are you happy now?"

"Get away from me, you puke. Don't patronize me, you coward."

Lucifer ran over to Marie and took her in a chokehold. He began to run towards an exit. Marie stomped on his foot.

"Ow, you bitch!"

She broke away. The Zulu warriors charged Lucifer and threw him to the ground. He put up a fierce struggle and was about to break free until Rick came over and smashed him in the face again. Lucifer fell back, silenced. Behind the Zulus, a glowing figure appeared. It was a woman in a white gown with long dark hair. She came forward to stand beside the body of Lucifer. It was Margaret from the river of Contempt. She placed her hand over Lucifer's head. An intense white light entered into his body. She spoke softly, though all could hear.

"I am here to take this dark soul to the place of no return. He will be taken to the source of energy that becomes life. He has been unteachable and will never exist again."

They disappeared. The auditorium was silent.

Rick went up on the stage. "The elder spirits have asked me to speak to you." The audience settled down and listened. George and Marie found some chairs and were seated.

"Life on earth can and will go on if we work together. Find the God of your understanding. Pray to your God, which is generous and loving. The physical life is hard. It requires constant attention. Humans can do it. It is worth it. You are worth it."

Rick went to Luiza, and they both vanished.

EPILOGUE

Word spread after the meeting: an extraordinary change was underway. The Mideast conflict deescalated, avoiding further devastation. Leaders spoke, statements were published, and cooperation began to improve. Perhaps someone above was listening. A sense of hope took hold.

Marie returned to her family in Paris. George left for Spain, where his wife Maria awaited him.

The End

Author and wife Isabel Maria, 2024, in Spain.

References

[1] P. Michael Newton, Journey of Souls: Case Studies of Life Between Lives, Llewellyn Worldwide, Ltd.: Llewellyn Publications, 1994.

[2] P. Yogananda, Autobiography of a Yogi, New York: The Philosophical Library, 1946.

[3] University of Virginia Division of Persceptional Studies Videos, Books.

[4] Life After Life by Raymond Moody, MD 1967